W9-BHW-592

"I don't find you plain at all, Jessica. On the contrary, I find you quite irresistibly lovely."

Just for a second everything in the room seemed to hang in frozen tension. The pretty Christmas tree ornaments stopped twirling, the lights ceased their tiny reflective flickerings. Even the flames in the hearth grew still. She held on to that moment as long as she could, then came straight out and asked him, "Are you married, Morgan?"

"Not anymore."

"And do you find me intimidatingly sensible?"

"I don't intimidate that easily, Jessica."

"Then why haven't you tried to make love to me?"

CATHERINE SPENCER, once an English teacher, fell into writing through eavesdropping on a conversation about Harlequin Romance. Within two months she changed careers and sold her first book to Harlequin in 1984. She moved from England to Canada thirty years ago and has four grown children—two daughters and two sons—plus three dogs and a cat. In her spare time she plays the piano, collects antiques and grows tropical shrubs.

Books by Catherine Spencer

Don't miss any of our special offers. Write to us at the following address for information on our newest releases.

Harlequin Reader Service
U.S.: 3010 Walden Ave., P.O. Box 1325, Buffalo, NY 14269
Canadian: P.O. Box 609, Fort Erie, Ont. L2A 5X3

CATHERINE SPENCER

Christmas with a Stranger

Harlequin Books

TORONTO • NEW YORK • LONDON
AMSTERDAM • PARIS • SYDNEY • HAMBURG
STOCKHOLM • ATHENS • TOKYO • MILAN
MADRID • WARSAW • BUDAPEST • AUCKLAND

If you purchased this book without a cover you should be aware
that this book is stolen property. It was reported as "unsold and
destroyed" to the publisher, and neither the author nor the
publisher has received any payment for this "stripped book."

ISBN 0-373-11927-5

CHRISTMAS WITH A STRANGER

First North American Publication 1997.

Copyright © 1997 by Catherine Spencer.

All rights reserved. Except for use in any review, the reproduction or
utilization of this work in whole or in part in any form by any electronic,
mechanical or other means, now known or hereafter invented, including
xerography, photocopying and recording, or in any information storage
or retrieval system, is forbidden without the written permission of the
publisher, Harlequin Enterprises Limited, 225 Duncan Mill Road,
Don Mills, Ontario, Canada M3B 3K9.

All characters in this book have no existence outside the imagination of
the author and have no relation whatsoever to anyone bearing the same
name or names. They are not even distantly inspired by any individual
known or unknown to the author, and all incidents are pure invention.

This edition published by arrangement with Harlequin Books S.A.

® and TM are trademarks of the publisher. Trademarks indicated with
® are registered in the United States Patent and Trademark Office, the
Canadian Trade Marks Office and in other countries.

Printed in U.S.A.

PROLOGUE

HE WAS on the outside again. On the run. Eventually, of course, they'd catch up with him, and when they did they'd put him away for an even longer stretch. But meanwhile time was on his side. Time in which to carry out the plan he'd spent nine years perfecting. Time to exact punishment for the injustice meted out to him.

Oh, he'd been a model inmate! So clever, fooling all of them with the mealy-mouthed responses they'd wanted to hear. So eager to be rehabilitated, so willing to admit the error of his ways. Oozing humility and remorse enough to make a thinking man's stomach revolt.

But they weren't thinking men, they were fools. Fools and tools of the system that had rejected him—except for the man who'd put him behind bars. *He* was an adversary worth taking on. Outwitting *him* would be a triumph, something in which to take delight when they caught up with him again.

What else, after all, had he to nourish his soul? No wife, certainly, and a child who called some stranger "Father". No home, no job. And no future. Model prisoner or not, his past would go with him wherever he went. For the rest of his life.

It was the way things were done these days. Forget all that nonsense about a man having paid for his crimes. He never wrote off the debt because they plastered his face and name on community notice boards and labeled him a dangerous offender, even if he'd been judged guilty of only one crime—and that vindicated in the eyes of God-fearing people.

5

Vermin, that was what he'd stamped out. A temptation of the devil's making best wiped off the face of the earth. A cheap flirt dolled up to look like decent folk, preying on a man's weakness when he was most vulnerable. Reaching across his desk in such a way that he was filled with the scent of her.

It would have been different if he'd been allowed his conjugal rights, but Lynn had refused him ever since she'd almost lost the baby in her fifteenth week. That had left nearly six months during which he'd been denied his husbandly prerogative. Small wonder he'd fallen victim to the other woman's wiles.

He hadn't meant to kill her. It had been an accident— a panic reaction. She'd made a scene when he'd told her he wouldn't leave his wife for her, and threatened to phone his home, to tell Lynn what a louse she had for a husband, and for a few blind moments he'd lost control and it had just…happened.

He might have been acquitted—at worst found guilty of nothing more heinous than aggravated assault resulting in death. The judge had seemed inclined to sympathy at times, and the jury might have found in his favor—if it hadn't been for Morgan Kincaid.

Kincaid was the one who'd taken everything away and left him with nothing to lose.

Well, Merry Christmas, Mr. Crown Prosecutor!

It was payback time.

CHAPTER ONE

THE snow began in earnest just as darkness fell. Dense, feathery flakes whirling across the beam of her headlights to imprison her in a closed and isolated world.

Jessica hadn't been comfortable with the driving conditions from the start. She was used to a milder sort of winter on the island, one of west coast sea mist and wind-driven rain, not the breath-freezing cold of the high Canadian interior.

She'd spent last night in a small town tucked between a lake and the highway, in a country inn built to resemble a Swiss chalet. There'd been logs blazing in the fireplace in the lobby and a twelve-foot Christmas tree that filled the air with the scent of pine, and French onion soup smothered in melted cheese for dinner. It had been a warm, safe place now some three hundred miles behind—much too far to merit her turning back.

If she wanted shelter from the weather again tonight, her only option was to tackle the eighty miles of switchback mountain road that lay between her and her next stop on the way to Whistling Ridge.

Smearing a gloved hand across the windshield, she squinted through the swirling snow, her heart lurching as the wheels of the car skidded suddenly to the right. Upright poles planted at intervals to measure the depth of the winter snowfall were all that stood between her and the swift, steep drop to the valley below.

This was insanity and only the fact that Selena had been injured in a ski-lift accident could have induced her to abandon her original holiday plans and embark on such a journey. But then, wasn't that how it had always been, ever since they were children? With Selena getting into trouble of one kind or another, and Jessica dropping everything to come to the rescue?

Another forty-five-degree bend loomed up ahead. Cautiously, she steered into the turn. Halfway around, she saw the flicker of headlights below her as another driver navigated the road, but more quickly, with an assurance she sorely lacked.

Once on the straight again, she increased her speed. She had little choice. The car behind was gaining rapidly, there was no room to pass and the snow was, if anything, falling more thickly. In great fat clumps the size of footballs, in fact, that rolled down the mountainside and bounced across the road.

Headlights dazzled in her rear-view mirror. A horn blared, repeatedly, furiously. Panic choked her throat. Was the other driver mad? Trying to run her off the road?

All at once, the open mouth of an avalanche shed yawned blackly a few yards in front, offering a brief haven of safety where she could let whoever was in such a hurry behind get past her.

Clutching the steering wheel in a death grip, Jessica pressed down on the accelerator and shot into the shelter with the other vehicle practically nosing her bumper from behind.

And then the air was filled with thunder and the earth seemed to rock beneath her. And the road, which was supposed to run all the way to Whistling Valley ski resort where Selena lay in a hospital bed, came to a sudden end at the far end of the avalanche shed.

At first Jessica didn't believe it and, pulling as far over to one side as possible to allow the other driver to get by, kept her car idling forward. Until she saw that there was no way out of the shed, that its exit truly was blocked by a wall of snow, and that, far from trying to pass her, her pursuer had drawn to a stop also, and was climbing out of his vehicle and coming toward her.

Incongruously large and implicitly threatening in the light cast by his car's headlamps, his shadow leaped ahead of him on the concrete wall of the shed. Reaching for the control panel on the console, Jessica snapped the doors locked and wished she could as easily subdue the tremor of apprehension racing through her.

Approaching her window, he stooped and stared in at her. She had the impression of a man perhaps in his early forties; of dark displeasure, well-defined brows drawn together in a scowl, and a mouth paralleling the same vexation. Of wide shoulders made all the more imposing by the bulky jacket he wore, and of masculine power composed not just of sinew but of command, as though he was not inclined to tolerate having his authority thwarted by anyone.

The way he rapped on her window and ordered, "Open it," bore out the idea, especially when she found herself automatically obeying the directive and lowering the glass an inch.

"Do you have a death wish?" The question blasted toward her on a cloud of frosty air.

Unvarnished disapproval laced the husky baritone of his voice, leaving her in no doubt that she was alone with a stranger who looked and sounded very much as if he'd like to take her neck between his powerful hands and wring it.

But she wasn't earning accolades as the youngest headmistress ever appointed to Springhill Island's Private School for Girls by cowering in the face of incipient trouble. "Certainly not," she said, as calmly as her thudding heart would allow. "But I imagine you must, if the way you were driving is any indication. You practically ran me off the road."

For a moment she thought she'd managed to silence him. His jaw almost dropped and he appeared to be at a loss for words. He shook his head, as though unsure that he'd heard her correctly, then recovered enough to say, "Lady, do you have the foggiest idea what's just happened?"

"Of course." She gripped the steering wheel more firmly. It was easier to keep her hands from shaking that way. "There has been a bit of a snow slide."

"There has been a bloody avalanche," he informed her with a rudeness she would not for a moment have tolerated in her students. "And if you'd had your way we'd both be buried under a load of snow—always assuming, of course, that we hadn't been swept clear down the mountain."

Embarrassingly, her teeth started to chatter with shock then, and short of stuffing both gloved hands in her mouth, there was little she could do to disguise the fact except blurt out, "That must be why it's so cold in here."

At that, he straightened up and thumped a fist on the roof of her car, sending a clump of snow slithering down her windshield. "I don't believe what I'm hearing," he informed the shed at large, his words echoing eerily. "Is this her way of trying to be funny?"

"Hardly," she retorted, addressing the zippered front of his down jacket, which was all she could see of him. "I plan to spend tonight in Wintercreek and have quite a few miles still to cover before I get there. I'd just as soon not waste time keeping you entertained with witticisms."

He bent down to confront her again, squatting so that his face was on a level with hers. "Let me get this straight. You expect to reach Wintercreek tonight?"

"Didn't I just say as much?" She wished she could see his face more clearly. But everything about him was a little bit distorted in the flare of his car's headlamps, with one side of his features thrown into dark relief and the other silhouetted in light. Like opposite sides of a coin—or good and evil all wrapped up in one package.

She suppressed a shudder. This was not the time for such fanciful notions. It was a time for positive thought and action. "I have a hotel reservation—"

"I heard you the first time and I hope your deposit's refundable," he interrupted curtly. "Because, as they say in the vernacular of these parts, 'honey, you ain't goin' nowhere any time soon'."

"Are you telling me I'm stuck in here until someone comes to rescue me?"

"That's what I'm telling you."

Her confidence nosedived a little further. "And…um…how long do you think that will take?"

He shrugged. "Hard to say. First light tomorrow, if we're lucky."

"But that's almost twelve hours away!"

"I know." He braced his hands against his knees and shoved himself upright again. "Better turn off the engine before you asphyxiate us, and resign yourself to sleeping in your back seat. Open the trunk and I'll hand in your emergency supplies."

She hadn't thought it possible for anything to make her heart sink any lower but, to her dismay, he managed it with his last remark. "Emergency supplies?"

"Sleeping bag, candle, GORP."

"GORP?" she echoed faintly.

"Good old raisins and peanuts. Trail mix, cereal bars, stuff to keep your stomach from folding in on itself—call it what you like; I don't care. Let's just get you settled before we both die of exposure."

"I don't… I have only a suitcase. With clothes in it," she added, as if that might mitigate things a little.

It didn't. Thumping a fist on the roof of her car yet again, he let out a long, irritable exhalation. "I might have known!"

"Well, I didn't," Jessica said tartly. "They never

mentioned an avalanche on the weather report. If they had, I'd have stayed off the road. And please stop bludgeoning my car like that. Things are quite bad enough without your making them any worse.''

She thought he swore then. Certainly he muttered something unfit to be repeated in mixed company. Eventually, he composed himself enough to order, "Get out of the car.''

"And go where? You already said no one's likely to rescue us tonight.''

"Get out of the car. Unless you were lying a moment ago and you really do harbor a death wish.''

"I'd just as soon—''

"Get out of the goddamned car!''

It was Jessica's strongly held belief that a teacher who wished to retain control of her classes should make clear her expectations at the outset. Insubordination ranked high on her list of priorities. Unless it was stamped out at the start, it flourished quickly and completely undermined a teacher's authority. Related to that were the social graces which, in her opinion, were as important a part of the curriculum as any other subject. She felt it was incumbent on her and her staff to teach by example wherever possible.

Which was why, when she replied to her companion's incivility, she resisted the temptation to tell him to take a flying leap into the nearest snow bank and, instead, said firmly but politely, "I'll do no such thing. Furthermore, I don't like your tone.''

"I don't like anything about this situation,'' he shot back, singularly uncowed. "Believe me, if finding myself stranded overnight was in the cards when I got out of bed this morning, I can think of a dozen people I'd rather keep company with than some ditsy woman who doesn't have the brains to travel equipped for winter driving conditions.''

"I'm not seeking your company,'' Jessica snapped.

"But you're stuck with it," he said, chafing his bare hands together to keep the circulation going and turning toward his own vehicle again. "So hop out of the car *now*, because it's not big enough for two to stretch out in and I'd like to get some sleep."

Horrified, Jessica stared at him as the import of his words struck home. "You expect me to spend the night in your car...with you?"

"It beats the alternative," he said bluntly. "Life's tough enough without my waking up tomorrow to find a frozen corpse on my hands"

"But—!"

He blew into his cupped palms and, with the first hint of humor he'd shown so far, slewed an alarming leer her way. "Listen, we can debate the propriety of the arrangement once we're under the covers."

He was rude and he was outrageous—but, she was beginning to realize, he was right on one score at least. The cold was seeping through the open window to infiltrate her clothing most unpleasantly.

Still, she wasn't about to cave in to his suggestions without a murmur. "I think I should warn you that I have taken several courses in self-defense."

"Pity you didn't start worrying about your safety before now," he said, his expression at once resuming its former forbidding aspect. "As it happens, I'm harmless, but it would well serve you right if— Oh, what the hell!"

He pushed himself away from her car and seemed to make a concerted effort to rein in the anger suddenly vibrating around him. "You've got five minutes to make up your mind. If you're not out of this car and into mine by the time I've got my sleeping bag unfolded, better say your prayers and write out your last will and testament, because, lady..." he blew into his hands again to emphasize his point "...it'll be the last thing you ever do."

And with that he marched back to his car and doused the headlamps, leaving only hers to bathe the shelter in their glow. She heard a door slam, another open. Saw an interior light go on as he rummaged around at the back of what appeared to be a large utility vehicle. And knew, as the chill already invading the inside of her car crept deeper into her limbs, that she had little choice about what to do next.

He could be a serial killer, a deranged psychopath, a man intent on choking the living breath out of her, but, if she chose to ignore his less than gracious invitation, she'd wind up dead by the morning anyway.

Swallowing doubts and reservations along with what was left of her pride, she rolled up the window and stepped out of the car. As though crouching in wait for just such an ill-prepared victim, the cold took serious hold, knifing through her mohair winter coat as if it were made of nothing more substantial than silk.

Just as she approached, her reluctant knight jumped down from the tailgate of his vehicle, which turned out to be a Jeep whose heavy winter tires were looped with snow chains. "Smart decision," he said, shrugging free of his jacket. "Take off your boots and coat, then hop in."

She liked to think she'd outgrown any tendency toward foolish impulse and indeed spent a good portion of her tenure as headmistress counseling her students to think before they spoke, to temper spontaneity with deliberation. Yet the question was out of her mouth before she could prevent it, gauche and horribly suggestive. "Why do we have to take off our clothes if all we're going to do is sleep?"

He stood before her, the interior light of the Jeep enhanced by the glow of a candle set in a tin can on the floor under the dashboard. Quite enough illumination for her to take in the powerful breadth of shoulder beneath the heavy jacket and lean, athletic hips snugly clad in blue jeans. Was it also enough for him to detect the sweep of color that flooded her face?

If it was, he chose to ignore the fact, instead pointing out what would have been painfully obvious to anyone of sound mind. "I stand six three in my bare feet. Last time I checked, I weighed in at a hundred and ninety-four pounds. For that reason I bought an extra-large sleeping bag but it's still going to be a snug fit for two. I no more want your snowy boots in the small of my back than you want mine in yours. As for the coat, you might want to roll it up and use it as a pillow."

"Of course," she muttered, chagrined. "How stupid of me."

"Indeed!" He rolled his eyes and gestured her toward the Jeep with a flourish. "Climb aboard, stash your boots in the corner, and make yourself comfortable."

Comfortable? Not in a million years, Jessica thought, trying to keep her sweater in place as she slithered into the sleeping bag.

No sooner was she settled than he slammed closed the tailgate and raised the rear window, rather like a jailer securing a prison cell. He then went around to the driver's door, pulled it closed behind him, shucked off his boots and, tossing his jacket ahead of him, proceeded to crawl over the seat and join her in the back of the Jeep.

Inching into the sleeping bag, he turned on his side so that his back was toward her. Why couldn't she have left it at that? What demon of idiocy compelled her to try to make pillow talk?

Yet, "This is really quite absurd," she heard herself remark, in a voice so phonily arch that she cringed.

He sort of shifted his shoulders around and tugged his folded jacket into a more comfortable position beneath his head. "How so?"

"Well, here we are in bed together, and we don't even know each other's names."

"Uh-huh."

"I'm Jessica Simms."

"Are you?" he said indifferently. "Well, goodnight, Jessica Simms."

As snubs went, that rated a ten. "Goodnight," she replied huffily, and went to turn her back on him. Except that, now that he was hogging most of the sleeping bag, there really wasn't room for such maneuvering, a fact he was quick to point out.

"Quit fidgeting and nest up against me," he said impatiently. "Every time you shuffle around like that, you let in cold air."

"Nest?" she quavered, refusing to allow the import of "up against me" to take visual hold in her mind.

"Like two spoons, one around the other."

And just in case she hadn't understood he reached back one arm and yanked her close so that her breasts were flattened next to his spine and her pelvis cradled his buttocks. Truly a most compromising situation and one she could only be thankful none of her colleagues or students was likely to hear about.

"Thank you," she said politely. "You're very kind."

She felt his sigh, rife with exasperation and heartfelt enough that it lifted the sleeping bag and let out a little gust of warm air. "For crying out loud, go to sleep," he said.

Of course, it was an order impossible to obey—for him as well as for her, at least to begin with. For the longest time, he lay next to her, long, strong and tense as steel. But gradually, as the night progressed, his muscles relaxed, and she must have dozed off herself because the next time she became aware of her surroundings he was sleeping on his stomach with his face turned toward her.

In the steady light of the candle, she saw that he was not as old as she'd first supposed and looked to be only in his late thirties. It was fatigue that etched his face, carving deep lines beside his mouth and between his eyes, and making him appear older.

Even as she watched, he seemed to sink further into sleep, so that the grooves relaxed, then faded away until she had nothing left to look at but his long, silky lashes touching softly against the lean austerity of his cheekbones.

How handsome he was, she thought.

What colour were his eyes?

Dreamy brown? No, he was not the dreamy type.

Icy green? Possibly. Despite the warmth generated by his body, she sensed that he was a cool, reserved man. Cold, even.

Her arm had grown numb from being cramped beneath her. She flexed her fingers and, with excruciating care, slid her wrist out and across her waist. But cautiously, without creating the least little draft, so that not even the candle flame wavered.

His eyes flew open anyway, alert and noticeably blue, and caught her staring.

Was the spark of sexual awareness that blazed briefly between him and her a figment of her imagination?

"What?" he muttered, the word laced with suspicion, and she decided that, yes, it must have been her imagination.

"Nothing. My arm—" She levered the rest of it free and waggled her fingers, wincing at the pins and needles trying to paralyze them. "It went to sleep."

"Pity you didn't," he said, his head with its thick, dark hair lowering again to the makeshift pillow.

As suddenly as he'd woken, he fell asleep again. She shivered, less from the cold air lurking around them than from the stark lack of sympathy she sensed in him. She was inconveniencing him terribly, no doubt about it, and even less welcome in his sleeping bag than a bed bug.

Selena's latest crisis couldn't have come at a more inappropriate time, Jessica thought uncharitably. By now

she should be lounging beneath a sun umbrella in balmy
Cancun and trying to pretend she was more than a
lonely, thirty-year-old woman most of whose dreams
seemed unlikely to come true, not risking life and limb
to be with a sister who had little use for her except when
disaster arose.

But the avalanche wasn't Selena's fault; nor was it
hers. And if her sleeping partner thought their present
arrangement was inconvenient, how much worse would
he have found it if she'd sped through the shed fast
enough to wind up trapped under the snow at the other
end? Or would he have left her to her fate and gone
calmly about the business of making himself comfortable for the night without sparing her a thought?

Remembering how irritably he'd reacted to her lack
of preparedness, she suspected he'd have left her to suf-
focate. It irked her enough to want to punish him,
enough for her to make no attempt at stealth or silence
when she struggled to her other side so that she was
facing the deep perpendicular embrasures of the snow
shed and no longer tempted to look at him.

He reacted with the same ill temper he'd displayed
before. "For Pete's sake settle down," he grumbled.
"You're worse than a pair of puppies wrestling in a
gunny sack."

And again, just as before, he ensured her compliance
by anchoring her in place, but this time so that he was
snugly cushioned against her behind, and one of his
long, strong legs pinned down hers, and she could feel
his breath on the back of her neck.

It was an exceedingly…intimate situation.

Exceedingly!

Her watch showed ten minutes past eight when she
awoke to find herself alone in the back of the Jeep. A
fresh candle burned in the tin can under the dashboard
and the start of another day seeped through the upper

sections of the narrow vents on the downhill side of the shed to cast a pale, chill light along its length. Pushing herself into a sitting position and finger-combing loose strands of hair back from her face, Jessica saw him coming toward her from the far end of the tunnel.

Quickly, she shuffled free of the sleeping bag and pulled her clothing into place. By the time he hauled open the tailgate, she had her boots on and looked as respectable as could be expected, given the circumstances.

"Have they come to rescue us?" she asked, putting on her coat.

"No." He reached under the dashboard on the passenger side of the Jeep and pulled out a small knapsack.

"Then what were you doing at the end of the shed?"

He handed her a foil-wrapped cereal bar and raised his dark, level brows wryly. "Same thing you'll probably want to do before much longer," he remarked pointedly.

To say that she blushed at that would have been the understatement of the century. She felt herself awash in a tide of pure scarlet. "Oh...yes—I...um...I...see what you mean."

"Don't let modesty get the better of you. The sun's barely up and I don't hold out much hope of us being dug out for at least another half hour. Too risky for the highway crew, when they can't see what the conditions are like up the mountain. And that's always assuming that there isn't three feet of snow blocking the road between them and us."

Jessica's gaze swung to the nearest embrasure beyond which the narrow strip of sky now showed the palest tint of pink. "And if there is?" She could barely bring herself to voice the question. The thought of being imprisoned another day with him and with such a total lack of privacy didn't bear contemplating.

"We might be here until mid-morning. Possibly even

longer. It'd take a bulldozer to cut a path through anything that deep.'' He hitched one hip on the tailgate and
swung one long, blue-jeaned leg nonchalantly, as if picnic breakfasts in avalanche sheds were an entirely usual
part of his weekly routine. ''So, Jessica Simms, want to
tell me what persuaded you to drive up here with nothing
more reliable than a set of all-weather radials and a road
map to get you where you're going?''

''I'm on my way to visit my sister in Whistling
Valley.''

''That's another seven hours' drive away. You'd better stop in Sentinel Pass and get yourself outfitted with
a set of decent tire chains if you seriously want to get
there in one piece.''

''Yes.'' She squirmed under his scrutiny, aware that
while he seemed to be learning quite a bit about her she
knew next to nothing about him. ''You haven't told me
your name yet.''

''Morgan. If you knew you were coming up here for
Christmas, why the hell didn't you plan ahead? BCAA
or any travel agency could have warned you what sort
of conditions to expect.'' He took another bite of his
breakfast bar, then added scathingly, ''Maybe then you'd
have chosen clothing more appropriate than that flimsy
bit of a coat and those pitiful excuses for winter boots
you're currently wearing.''

He was worse than a pit bull, once he got his teeth
into something. Clearly, he found her apparent incom-
petence morbidly fascinating. ''I didn't have time to plan
ahead, Mr. Morgan. This trip came about very suddenly.''

''I see.'' He crushed the wrapping from his breakfast
into a ball, tossed it, backhanded, into the open knapsack
and unearthed a bottle of mineral water.

She shook her head as he unscrewed the cap and offered her a drink. She wasn't about to let a drop of liquid
past her lips until she was assured of more civilized

washroom facilities. It was all very well for a man to make do but for a woman....

"Some sort of family emergency?"

"What?"

"This sudden decision to visit your sister, was it—?"

"Oh!" She tucked her hands into the pockets of her coat and hunched her shoulders against the cold, which seemed even more pervasive than it had been the night before. "Yes. She hurt her back in a ski-lift accident and at first it seemed that her injuries were serious."

"But now that you're up to your own neck in trouble they don't seem so bad?"

"No," Jessica retorted, bristling at the implied criticism. "I phoned the hospital again before I left the hotel yesterday and learned her condition's been upgraded to satisfactory." She sighed, exasperation adding to the tension already gripping her. "It's just that Selena's always been prone to getting herself into difficulties of one kind or another."

"Must run in the family," he said mockingly, and took another swig of the water.

She was spared having to field his last observation by the rumble of a heavy engine outside the east end of the shed.

He shoved away from the tailgate and recapped the bottle. "Sounds as if the rescue squad have made it through already. Couldn't have been much of a slide, after all."

They were heaven-sent words.

"Thank goodness!" She scrambled down after him. "And thank you, Mr. Morgan. You undoubtedly saved my life and I'm very grateful."

"I undoubtedly did, Miss Jessica, and you're welcome."

"Have a very merry Christmas."

She thought perhaps a shadow crossed his face then,

but all he said was, "No need to race back to your car. It'll take a while before they clear a way out for us."

"It's a miracle to me that they even knew where to come looking."

"They have sensors strung all along the vulnerable stretches of highway. The minute one gets wiped out, they know there's been a slide and they usually don't waste much time getting to it."

"I see." She pulled the collar of her coat more snugly around her neck. "Well, I think I'll wait in my car, just the same. The cold's making its presence felt again."

"As you like." He closed the tailgate and raised the rear window of the Jeep. "Just don't fire up your engine until we see daylight. Wouldn't want to die from carbon monoxide poisoning when we've made it this far, would we?"

"I'm well aware of the danger from exhaust fumes, Mr. Morgan," she said loftily, resenting his confident assumption that, because she'd been ill prepared to cope with an avalanche, she must be some sort of congenital idiot.

Half an hour later, however, she was half convinced his assessment might not be far wrong. By then enough passage had been cleared for one of the road crew to come into the shed to check on its occupants.

"Start her up, ma'am," he said kindly, stopping at her window. "You'll be on your way in about ten minutes, but you might as well be warm while you wait."

After a bit of coaxing, her car sputtered to life and shortly after she heard the roar of the Jeep's engine. Outside, she could see that although the sun had not yet risen above the surrounding mountains the sky was such an intense blue that its reflection trapped hints of mauve in the snow heaped up along the road.

Perhaps if she hadn't been so mesmerized by the sight of freedom she'd have noticed sooner that her troubles were far from at an end. Only when one of the road crew waved her forward did she switch her attention to her car and see the red warning light on her dashboard.

Instinct led her to do exactly the right thing and switch off the car's ignition immediately. The damage, however, was already done, as evidenced by the puff of steam escaping from under the hood.

Behind her the Jeep's horn blasted impatiently, but even a fool could have seen that her car wasn't going anywhere.

With mounting dismay, Jessica watched as her sleeping companion jumped down from the Jeep, exasperation and resignation evident in every line of him, and, in a dismaying rerun of last night's fiasco, approached her window.

"Don't tell me," he jeered, coming to a halt beside her. "Either you've forgotten how to take your foot off the brake or your damned car's broken down."

CHAPTER TWO

ANY hopes Jessica might have entertained that the extent of the problem was not too serious the almighty Mr. Morgan quickly put to rout.

He surveyed her engine, which continued to puff out little clouds of steam like a mini-volcano on the verge of erupting. "It figures," he drawled, rolling his eyes heavenward, and beckoned the road crew to come see for themselves the latest misfortune she'd brought down on her hopelessly inept head.

"Release the hood," one of them called out to her, and, after they had it propped open, they clustered around the innards of her car with the rapt attention all men seemed to foster for such things. There followed a muttered discussion to which Jessica, still slumped disconsolately behind the steering wheel, was not privy.

Eventually, the Morgan man came back and leaned one elbow on the roof. "Might as well face it, Jessica Simms," he announced conversationally, his voice floating through the window which she'd opened a crack. "The only way this puddle-hopper's going to move is hitched to the back end of a tow truck."

She could have wept, with disappointment, frustration, and rage. "I suppose," she said, hazarding what seemed like a reasonable guess, "that my radiator's overheated?"

"On the contrary, it's frozen. Better phone your sister and tell her not to expect you at her bedside any time soon. Sentinel Pass is the nearest place you'll find a service station and they're working around the clock to

24

keep emergency vehicles on the road. Types like you go to the bottom of their list of priorities.''

He bent down and pinned her with a disparaging blue stare. ''Of course, all this could have been avoided if you'd used the brains God gave you and taken your car in for winter servicing.''

''I intended to,'' she spat, terribly afraid that if she allowed herself a moment's weakness she'd burst into tears instead. ''The moment school was out for the holidays I planned to go over to the mainland and have it attended to. Normally, it's something I take care of earlier, but we've had such a mild winter so far this year—''

''Ah, well,'' he interrupted, with patently insincere sympathy, ''they do say the road to hell is paved with good intentions, don't they?''

''Oh, put a sock in it!'' she retorted, consigning good manners to perdition, along with any remnant of seasonal goodwill toward him that she might have been inclined to nurture.

If Satan had chosen that moment to take human form and torment a woman past endurance, he would have smiled exactly as Mr. Morgan smiled then. With devastating, dazzling delight.

A couple of the road crew joined him at the window. ''We're about ready to head back to Sentinel Pass, Mr. Kincaid, so if you want a hand pushing the car over to the side...?''

''I'd appreciate it,'' he said. ''Get Stedman's to phone once they've towed it in and had a chance to assess the damage, will you? As for you,'' he barked, stabbing an imperious finger in Jessica's direction, ''we've frozen our butts off long enough on your account. Into the Jeep, fast, and don't bother to argue or complain!''

She had no inclination to do either. Her most pressing need was to find a washroom in the not too distant future, so the sooner they arrived at wherever he was taking her the better. But he offered not a word of explanation of where that might be as he drove out of the snow shed and, some five miles further along the highway, turned north onto a narrow road that twisted snakelike up the side of the mountain.

As warmth from the heater blasted around her ankles, however, the frozen dismay of Jessica's situation began to melt enough for her to venture to ask, "Where are we going?"

"To my lair in the hills where I plan to have my wicked way with you," he said. "And if you don't like that scenario I'm willing to settle for driving you to the top of the hill and shoving you over the edge."

"Very funny, I'm sure," she said, refusing to let him rattle her, "but if that's all you have in mind you could have finished me off last night."

"Don't think the idea didn't occur to me," he warned, and swung left up an even narrower road so suddenly that her suitcase, which he'd flung in the back of the Jeep, rolled onto its side and landed with a thud against the wheel well.

"I think we would both much prefer it if I spent the day at the nearest hotel," she replied. "Perhaps where my car's going, and while it's being fixed I could freshen up and—?"

"There isn't any accommodation to be had in Sentinel Pass. It's a truck stop, not a tourist spot, and they're busy enough without having you underfoot all day. The closest town of any size is Wintercreek which you already know lies two hours east of here, so, like it or not, we're stuck with each other's company until you've got wheels again." He drew an irate breath. "Which will hopefully be later this afternoon."

Jessica swallowed a sigh and stared through the windshield. Thick stands of pine hemmed the road; directly ahead a snow-covered peak reared majestically into the clear sky. "Do you really have a home up here?" she asked doubtfully, afraid that, unless they arrived very soon, she was going to have to suffer yet another indignity and request that he pull over so that she could make a trip behind a tree. "It seems a very isolated place."

"That's what gives it its charm, Jessica. No nosy neighbors, no TV, just peace and quiet in which to do whatever I please—as a rule, that is."

"But you do have a phone service. I heard you tell the men who dug us out that whoever repairs my car should phone you when it's ready."

"We have the bare necessities," he allowed.

We? "So you don't live alone, then?"

"I don't live alone."

"I noticed," she said, when he showed no inclination to offer any further details, "that the road crew called you Mr. Kincaid, but you told me your name was Morgan."

"It is," he said. "Morgan Kincaid."

She swiveled to face him. "Then why did you let me make a fool of myself calling you Mr. Morgan?"

He flung her another satanic grin and she couldn't help noticing that, loaded with unholy malice though it was, it showcased a set of enviably beautiful teeth. "Because you do it so well, with such strait-laced gullibility."

He wasn't the first man in her life to have realized that, she thought grimly. Stuart McKinney had beaten him to it by a good seven years, and made a bigger fool of her than Morgan Kincaid could ever hope to achieve. "Then I'm happy I was able to provide you with a little entertainment," she replied. "It eases my guilt at having caused you so much inconvenience."

He swung the Jeep around a final bend and, approaching from the west, drove up a long slope which ended on a plateau sheltered by sheer cliffs at its northern edge. On the other fronts, open land sloped to a narrow valley with a river winding through, but it was not the view which left Jessica breathless so much as the house tucked in the lee of the cliffs.

Built of gray stone, with a steeply pitched slate roof, paned windows, chimney pots and verandas, it sprawled elegantly among the fir and pine trees, a touch of baronial England in a setting so unmistakably North American west that it should have been ludicrous, yet wasn't. It was, instead, as charming and gracious as it was unexpected.

To the left and a little removed from the main house stood a second building designed along complementary lines; a stable, Jessica guessed, whose upper floor served as another residence if the dark red curtains hanging at the windows were any indication. Smoke curled from the chimneys of both places and hung motionless in the still air, tangible confirmation that Morgan Kincaid hadn't lied when he'd claimed not to live alone.

"Okay, this is it," he said, drawing to a halt at the foot of a shallow flight of snow-covered steps in front of the main house.

Grabbing her suitcase, he led the way up to a wide, deep veranda and into a narrow lobby where he stopped and removed his boots. Jessica did likewise, then followed him into the toasty warmth of a vaulted entrance hall. Directly in front of her a staircase rose to a spindled gallery which ran the length of the upper floor.

"Go ahead, Jessica," Morgan Kincaid invited, his voice full of sly humor as he gestured up the stairs. "The bathroom's the first door to the right at the top. Take a shower while you're in there, if you like. You'll find towels in the corner cupboard next to the tub."

Beast! Fuming, Jessica grabbed her suitcase and scuttled off as fast as her stockinged feet would allow on the smoothly polished pine floorboards.

He waited until she'd disappeared before letting himself out of the house again and turning to the stables. Clancy was there, mucking out the stalls. Inhaling the pleasantly familiar scents of hay, fresh straw and horses, Morgan stood in the doorway and watched.

Without shifting his attention from the task at hand, Clancy spoke, his voice as rusted as an old tin can left out too long in the rain. "'Bout time you got here, Morgan. Expected you yesterday."

"I know," Morgan said, a picture of Jessica Simms' narrow, elegant figure rising clear in his mind. "I ran into a bit of trouble."

"Oh?" Clancy planted his pitchfork in a fresh pile of straw, rested one hand on the side of the stall and massaged the small of his back with the other. "How so?"

"Wound up spending the night in the avalanche shed just west of Sentinel Pass—with a woman. Her car's out of commission and she needs a place to stay until it's fixed, so I brought her here."

The smirk that had begun to steal over Clancy's weathered features at the start of Morgan's revelation disappeared into a scowl of alarm. "Lordy, Morgan, you got to get rid of her. This ain't a safe place for a woman right now."

"What's that supposed to mean?"

"Reckon you ain't been listening to the radio today, or you wouldn't be askin'. Reckon you ain't seen the mail I left in the main house, either. You got another Christmas card, Morgan. From Clarkville Penitentiary."

"The card I've come to expect," Morgan said, refusing to acknowledge the unpleasant current of tension that sparked the length of his spine at the mention of Clarkville, "but what do you mean about the news?"

"Gabriel Parrish broke out of jail late yesterday afternoon. Heard it on the seven o'clock broadcast this morning."

The tension increased perceptibly, although Morgan didn't let it show. "I'm surprised he's considered interesting enough to make the headlines."

"Heck, Morgan, there ain't a soul alive in British Columbia that don't remember his trial or the man who put him away. Reckon we'd see your face plastered right next to his on the TV, if we had one." Clancy cast him a speculative glance from beneath bushy brows. "How much you want to bet that he'll come lookin' for you, Mr. Prosecutor?"

"He'd be crazy to do that."

"There weren't never no question about his bein' crazy, Morgan. Real question is, is he crazy enough to come lookin' for revenge, and in my mind there ain't much doubt about it."

"Clarkville's hundreds of miles from here. The police will catch up with him soon enough, if they haven't already done so. He's no threat to me, Clancy."

"Get rid of the woman anyway, Morgan, unless you want to risk having her used for target practice."

"You spend too much time alone reading bad westerns," Morgan said. "Parrish isn't fool enough to come to the one place people might be expecting him. He's served nine of a twenty-five-year sentence. With time off for good behavior—and he's been a model prisoner by all accounts—he'd be eligible for parole in another six. He wouldn't blow everything now just to come after me." Morgan shook his head, as much to convince himself as Clancy. "No, he's looking for freedom, not a longer stretch behind bars."

"And what if he's got a different agenda, one that involves settling an old score? What then?"

"If it'll ease your mind any, I'll put in a call to the local police and let them know I'm spending Christmas here, just in case he shows up in the area." Morgan passed a weary hand across his eyes. "Beyond that, all I'm looking for is a hot shower, something rib-sticking to eat, and a nap. I didn't get much sleep last night."

"Do tell," Clancy squawked. "And wouldn't that just

curdle your ex's cream if she knew you'd found someone else to keep your feet warm in bed?''

"Don't let your imagination get the better of you,"
Morgan advised him sourly. "There's nothing going on
between me and Jessica Simms, I assure you. She's too
much an uptight copy of Daphne and I like to think I'm
smart enough not to fall for the same type twice.''

"Praise the Lord! Because, escaped con on the loose
or not as the case may be, this ain't no place for a
woman like that, Morgan, any more than you're the mar-
ryin' kind. Too wrapped up in your work, too short on
patience and too damned opinionated is what you are.
Women don't like that in a man.''

"You ought to know," Morgan said, laughing despite
the anxiety and irritation fraying the edges of his pleasure at being back at the ranch for the holidays. "Agnes
took on all three when she married you, and spent half
her life trying to cure you of them.''

Clancy pulled his worn old stetson down over his
brow and came to stand next to Morgan in the doorway.
"Had a little chat with her this mornin'," he murmured,
nodding to the enclosure atop a small rise beyond the
near meadow, where the ashes of his wife of forty-eight
years lay scattered. "Told her I'd put up a Christmas
tree in the main house, just like always. Remember all
the bakin' she used to do, Morgan, and the knittin' she
tried to hide, and all that business of hanging up a row
of socks, as if we was still kids believin' in Santa
Claus?''

"Of course I remember." Morgan slung an arm over
his shoulder, a gesture of affection which the hired hand
suffered reluctantly. "On Christmas Eve we'll light the
fire in the living room, raise a glass to her, and you'll
play the organ. She'd like to know we're keeping to the
traditions that meant so much to her.''

"Always assumin' we ain't been murdered in our
beds by then," Clancy said gloomily. "I'm tellin' you,

Morgan, Gabriel Parrish is *gonna* come lookin' for you. I feel it in my bones. And he ain't *gonna* knock at the front door and announce himself all nice and polite.''

Jessica heard the phone ring as she was toweling dry her hair. Heard, too, the muffled sound of Morgan Kincaid answering, although his exact words weren't clear.

When she came down the stairs a few moments later, she found him seated behind a heavy oak desk in a room which clearly served as some sort of office-cum-library, judging by the bookshelves lining the walls.

"The mechanic from the garage in Sentinel Pass just called," he said, bathing her in a glower. "Not only is your car radiator frozen solid, you've also got a cracked block."

There was no need to ask if he considered that to be bad news; his face said it all. "I gather it won't be fixed today, then."

"Not a chance," he said. "The earliest you'll be on your way is tomorrow—if you're lucky."

In Jessica's view, it was about time her luck changed for the better, but it didn't sound as if it was going to happen soon enough to please either of them. "And if I'm not? How long then?"

"It depends when they can get around to working on your car and how difficult it is to access the trouble. If they have to take out the engine...." His shrug sent a not unpleasant whiff of mountain air and stables wafting toward her. "You could be facing another day's delay."

"But that takes us right up to Christmas Eve! I can't possibly impose on you and your wife's hospitality for that length of time. No woman wants a stranger thrust on her at such a busy time of year. And my sister needs me."

"Your sister's going to have to get along without you a while longer," he declared, rolling the chair away from the desk and pacing moodily to the window. "And I don't have a wife."

"But you said...."

"I said I didn't live alone." He spun around to face her, his face a study in disgruntlement. "I did not say I was married."

"All the more reason for me to find some other place to stay, then," she blurted out, horrified to find her thoughts straying from the very pertinent facts of her dilemma with the car to the vague realization that she was afraid to be alone with this man.

He spelled danger, though why that particular word came to mind she couldn't precisely say. It had something to do with his sense of presence that went beyond mere good looks. Whatever it was, it had expressed itself in the middle of the night before and she knew it was only a matter of time before it would do so again. He exuded a complex and undeniable masculinity that she found...sexy.

An uncomfortable heat spread within her at the audacity of the admission. She did not deal with sexy; it had no relevance in her life. "I'm afraid," she said, "that you'll just have to drive me to Wintercreek yourself."

"Forget it," he said flatly. "Even if it didn't involve a three- or four-hour round trip for me, what good will it do you to be in one place when your car's in another, eighty miles away?"

Once again, he was so irrefutably *right* that, illogically, Jessica wanted to kick him. Curbing any such urge, she said, "In that case, I'll endeavor not to cause you any more trouble than I already have."

"You can do better than that," he said, and jerked his head toward a door at the far end of the main hall. "You can make yourself useful in the kitchen back there and set the table. There's a pot of chili heating on the wood-stove which should be ready to serve by the time I get cleaned up. Maybe a hot meal will leave us both more charitably inclined toward the other."

Confident that she'd obey without a qualm, he loped off, long legs moving with effortless rhythm up the stairs. Refusing to gaze after him like some star-struck ninth-grade student, Jessica made her way to the kitchen, which would have been hard to miss in a house twice as large.

Big and square, with copper pots hanging from the beamed ceiling and the woodstove he'd mentioned sending out blasts of heat, it could easily have accommodated a family of ten around the rectangular table in the middle of the floor, yet Morgan Kincaid clearly had the house pretty much to himself.

There'd been only one toothbrush in the bathroom, only one set of towels hanging on the rail, and an unmistakable air of emptiness in the row of closed doors lining the upper hall. Did he perhaps have a housekeeper who occupied the rooms above the stables? Was that what he'd meant when he'd said he didn't live alone?

If so, Jessica decided, taking down blue willow bowls and plates from a glass-fronted cabinet, she'd prefer spending the night with her, even if it meant sleeping on the floor. The favor of Morgan Kincaid's reluctant hospitality was no favor at all.

She was stirring the pot of chili set on a hot plate hinged to the top of the woodstove when a man of about seventy, accompanied by a pair of golden retrievers, came into the kitchen from a mud room off the enclosed porch at the back of the house.

Short, stocky and unshaven, his appearance was what one could most kindly call weathered. "You must be the woman," he observed from the doorway, unwinding a long, knitted scarf from around his neck and opening the buttons on a sheepskin-lined jacket.

Not quite sure how to respond to that, Jessica murmured noncommittally, replaced the lid on the chili pot, and bent to stroke the head of the smaller dog, who came to greet her before curling up in one of the two cushioned rocking chairs near the woodstove. The other animal remained beside his master and it was hard to tell which of the two looked more suspicious.

"You made any coffee?" the man inquired, in the same semi-hostile tone.

"Yes. May I pour you a cup?"

"Cup?" His gaze raked from her to the table and came to rest in outrage on the hand-sewn linen place mats and napkins she'd found in a drawer. "What the hell—? Who gave you the right to help yourself to Agnes's Sunday-best dishes and stuff?"

Compared to the acerbic dwarf confronting her now, Morgan Kincaid's personality suddenly struck Jessica as amazingly agreeable. She made no attempt to hide her relief when he, too, appeared and stood surveying the scene taking place, although she could have done without his smirk of amusement.

"Lookee, Morgan," the old buzzard with the dog spluttered furiously, "we got ourselves a woman with a nestin' instinct taking charge. Makin' herself right at home and pawin' through our private possessions as if she owns the place. Better watch yourself, or she'll be warmin' your bed again come nightfall."

"Put a lid on it," Morgan ordered him affectionately. "Jessica Simms, meet Clancy Roper, my hired hand. He looks after the horses when I'm not here, and keeps a general eye on the place. The dog in the chair is Shadow, the other's Ben. Clancy, this is the person I told you about whose car is being repaired."

"I didn't figure on her bein' the tooth fairy," Clancy returned. "How long you plannin' to keep her around, nosin' through the house and ferretin' out things that ain't any o' her concern?"

"Not a moment longer than necessary," Jessica informed him shortly, then pointedly addressed her next

remark to Morgan. "In addition to taking the unpardonable liberty of laying the table, I found a loaf of bread
and put it to warm in the oven. I hope that doesn't also
violate some unwritten rule of the house?"

"No," he said, a hint of apology merging with the
amusement dancing in his eyes. "And the table looks
very nice."

"In that case, if you're ready to eat I'll be happy to
dish up the food."

"I'm starving, and so must you be." He held out a
chair for her with a flourish that drew forth another irate
snort from the hired hand. "Have a seat and I'll take
over. We're used to doing for ourselves here, though not
quite as elegantly as this any more. Clancy, quit sulking
and sit down."

"The dogs needs feedin', or don't that matter now
that you got a woman trippin' you up every time you
turn round?"

"The dogs won't mind waiting." Unperturbed by the
irascible old man, Morgan set about serving the chili and
slicing the loaf of bread. "You want coffee with your
meal, Jessica, or would you prefer to have it afterward?"

"Whatever you're used to is fine with me."

"We usually have it with, especially during the winter
when the days are so short. We start bringing in the
horses around four in the afternoon, which doesn't allow
much time for a leisurely lunch."

"Ain't waitin' that long today," Clancy muttered,
practically swiping his flannel-shirted arm across the end
of Jessica's nose as he reached over to help himself to
bread. "Not only ain't the company the sort that makes
a man want to hang around, the sky's cloudin' up from
the north-east pretty damn fast. Reckon we'll be seein'
snow again before the day's out."

Morgan aimed a glance Jessica's way. "Just as well
you're not planning to drive all the way to Whistling
Valley today, after all, or you might be spending another

night on the road and leaving yourself at the mercy of the next person who happens to come along.''

"I'm really rather tired of your harping on about last night," she said, the note of reprimand in his remark really grating on her nerves. "I've already told you why I wasn't as well prepared for the weather as I would have been had circumstances been different, and I don't feel I owe you any further explanation or apology.''

"Right grateful little vixen, ain't she, Morgan?" Clancy Roper said gleefully. "Reckon that'll teach you not to go pickin' up strange women off the side of the highway."

"Doesn't it occur to you that you were lucky I was the one you found yourself trapped with?" Morgan lectured her, ignoring Clancy. "Or that you have a responsibility to yourself and society at large not to take that sort of risk with your safety?"

"I don't make a habit of expecting the worst," Jessica retorted. "Most people behave decently, I find, given the chance."

He spread long, lean fingers over the table top and shook his head. "Then you're kidding yourself. Good Samaritans are pretty thin on the ground these days, and just because it's Christmas doesn't mean you can afford to indulge in the wholesale belief that all men are full of goodwill.''

"Reckon we just might find that out the hard way," Clancy put in with a scowl, "if Gabriel—"

But before he could elaborate further Morgan cut him off with a meaningful glare and a brusque, "Shut up, Clancy. Let's not get into that again."

They ate the rest of the meal in strained silence. Once they were done, Morgan nodded to Clancy. "Feed the dogs while I bring in another load of wood," he said, heading for the back porch, "then we'll get back to the stables."

Feeling thoroughly superfluous, Jessica said, "Is there anything I can do to help?"

"Not unless you're used to working horses."

"Just got to look at her to see she wouldn't know the hind end of one if it was starin' her in the face," Clancy said, shoveling dog food into two bowls.

"You're right," Jessica informed him. "But I'm perfectly able to wash dishes and from the way you've managed to splatter chili all over yours it's just as well. I'm also capable of producing an acceptable evening meal."

"Lordy, Lordy," the old curmudgeon sneered back. "Ain't never before heard a woman spit out such a mouthful of hoity-toity words in one breath."

"Considering we're both lousy cooks," Morgan told him, "I think you'd be smart to button your lip. Jessica, feel free to take over the kitchen. There's a freezer full of stuff in the mud room, and sacks of potatoes and other vegetables. Oh, and help yourself to the phone in the office if you want to call the hospital again."

She did, and afterward almost wished she hadn't bothered. Selena, it turned out, had received a relatively minor injury to her spine—mostly bruising which, though painful, was not expected to create any lasting complications.

Jessica would have thought that was cause enough for any reasonable person to celebrate, but Selena was not famous for being reasonable. Thoroughly put out by the number of Christmas parties she was missing and the fact that the hospital restricted the number of visitors she was allowed, she devoted most of the conversation to a litany of complaint.

Patience stretched to the limit, Jessica finally cut short the call with the suggestion that since there was little Selena could do to change things she might as well make the most of them.

Such excellent advice, Jessica decided, hanging up the

phone, also applied to her. She found an apple pie and
a package of some kind of stewing meat that looked like
beef in the freezer, and potatoes, carrots and onions in
the vegetable bins. The refrigerator yielded up butter,
cheese, eggs, and a slab of back bacon. Jars of dried
herbs and such filled the shelves of a wooden spice rack.

By the time the snow that Clancy had predicted began
to fall, shortly after four, the kitchen was filled with the
rich aroma of meat and vegetables simmering in the
oven, the lunch dishes had been washed and returned to
their hallowed place in the glass-fronted cabinet, and
Jessica was left with nothing more pleasant to do than
await the return of her unwilling host and his uncivil
hired hand.

"Hardly the ideal dining companions," she commented to Shadow, who lifted her head sympathetically
from her spot in the rocker, then tucked her nose more
snugly under her tail.

The men came back about half an hour later. Their
footsteps clumped onto the back porch, followed shortly
thereafter by the door to the mud room being flung open
and the sound of something being dragged across the
floor.

"It'll dry out a bit overnight, and we'll put it up tomorrow," she heard Morgan Kincaid say. "Hang up
your jacket, and let's get inside where it's warm."

"Where the woman is, you mean," came the disagreeable reply.

"Well, Clancy," his employer drawled, in that husky,
come-hither sort of voice of his, "I'm willing to put up
with her company for another night if it means our coming in to find a good hot meal waiting on the table, and
after the sort of afternoon we've both put in I'd think
you would be too."

"Speak for yourself," Clancy snapped, clearly put out
by any such suggestion. "I'll make do the same as usual
when we ain't busy puttin' on our party hats for com-

pany we ain't asked for. A can of stew's good enough for me—in my own quarters with just Ben for company,'' he finished, ''and where I don't have to worry 'bout strangers pickin' through my stuff the minute my back's turned. See you in the mornin', boss.''

A low laugh rolled out of Morgan Kincaid. Low and, to a woman's ears at least, sexy. Jessica put both hands to her cheeks but was unable to control the flush of annoyance conjured up by yet another unwelcome interpolation of that word.

''Gee, thanks!'' he said. ''I'll remember this the next time it's my turn to do you a favor, old man. You know full well having her here isn't *my* idea of a good time, either.''

Pure anger left Jessica rooted to the spot. What did they think? That she *wanted* to be stranded here? Or that she was either too deaf to overhear their remarks or too stupid to understand them?

Well, Morgan Kincaid might like to think he knew what sort of evening lay in store for him, but he was about to discover it was going to be a lot worse than anything he could begin to imagine!

CHAPTER THREE

Morgan betrayed not a scrap of embarrassment when he came into the kitchen to find Jessica standing by the woodstove and well within earshot of anything said in the mud room. "Guess you heard that Clancy won't be joining us for dinner," he said, casually batting a few snowflakes from the inside of his collar where they must have strayed when he'd removed his jacket.

"That and a few other choice bits of conversation," Jessica replied stonily. "You've got a lot to learn about being a gracious host, Mr. Kincaid."

"Doubtless, but I'm not interested in taking a lesson right now." He nodded to the enamel coffee pot sitting on the stove top. "Any fresh coffee in there?"

"Find out for yourself," she said, amazed and shocked to hear his surliness rubbing off on her. "And, before you subject me to another homily on your munificence in having rescued me from a plight of my own making, allow me to point out that I have spent the afternoon trying to make up for some of the inconvenience I've put you to. There's fresh wood in the stove, dinner is ready whenever you are, the kitchen is clean—which is more than it was before—and all you have to do is relax and enjoy the evening.

"And," she concluded on a final, irate breath, "just in case I inadvertently say or do something to spoil the occasion, I'll be happy to take a tray up to whatever room you assign to me so that you're not forced to endure my unwelcome company a moment longer than necessary."

"Self-sacrifice doesn't suit you, Jessica," he snorted.

41

"As for your being unwelcome, let's face it, you're no more happy to be stranded here with me than I am to be saddled with you. This is my retreat, a place I enjoy specifically because it's nothing like..." he hesitated, and a grimace of distaste rippled over his expression "...the sort of world you undoubtedly prefer. I'm used to doing as I please up here, whenever it pleases me to do it."

Jessica sniffed disparagingly. "And what's that, exactly?"

"Whatever takes my fancy—going about unshaven and spending all day ankle-deep in horse manure, or rolling around naked in the snow if I feel like it, without having to worry that some puritanical biddy is going to go into cardiac arrest at the sight." He shrugged his big shoulders and unbuttoned the top two buttons of his wool shirt in what struck Jessica as a highly suggestive fashion, considering his last remark. "I find you a most inhibiting presence, Miss Simms."

Why, instead of reassuring her, did his words carry a sting that left her feeling drab and sexless? He was perfectly right, after all. She might be only thirty, but she typified the quintessential schoolmarm heading straight into cloistered spinsterhood, and wasn't that exactly the path she'd chosen for herself?

"I won't apologize for being who I am," she said briskly. "You'll simply have to control your unconventional urges until tomorrow when I'm gone. In the meantime, I'd appreciate your showing me to a room where I can spend the night."

"Oh, hell," he said, his husky drawl threaded with impatience, "help yourself to whichever one you please, as long as you don't choose mine."

As if having to share a bed with her two nights in a row was more than any red-blooded man should have to stomach! As if he'd rather sleep with a corpse!

Well, she'd known since she was sixteen that she was

no femme fatale. "Poor thing, your feet are your best feature," Aunt Edith had declared wearily, and had turned her attention as well as her affection on the far prettier Selena.

Did some of that old feeling of rejection seep through the indifferent facade Jessica had learned to present to the world? Was that what prompted Morgan Kincaid to add, with more kindness than he'd shown thus far in their relationship, "Hey, listen, I don't mean to come across as such a bear. I'm a bit preoccupied with other things, that's all. The room above the kitchen's the warmest, so why don't you throw your suitcase in there, then come down and join me for dinner? Go on," he urged, when she hesitated. "Whatever you've got cooking smells great and I promise I won't bite you by mistake."

It would have been churlish to refuse. Churlish, silly, and immature. Which explained why she nodded her agreement and made her way up the stairs to the room he'd singled out. Because she prided herself on being a mature, intelligent adult. It was one of the reasons why she'd achieved so much, so soon, in her career.

But how then did she justify the adolescent way she hurried to the mirror above the carved mahogany dressing table at the foot of the matching double bed and pulled the clasp out of her hair so that it flowed thick and full over her shoulders? As if such a simple change were enough to render her glamorous and alluring!

"You can't make a silk purse out of a sow's ear," Aunt Edith had maintained, and it was true. Men did less than look twice at thin, thirty-year-old women with slightly wavy brown hair and plain gray eyes; they didn't see them at all!

Jessica found her brush and drew it systematically through her hair until every strand lay smooth against her skull. With one hand she folded the customary loop at the nape of her neck, then with the other anchored it in place with a plain tortoiseshell barrette. She tucked her blouse more neatly into the waist of her navy pleated skirt and adjusted the starched points of her collar so that they paralleled the row of buttons aligned down the front of her meager chest.

She might not look better, but she looked familiar. And that left her feeling secure enough to brave an evening with Morgan Kincaid.

She walked with the upright, flowing grace of a nun, Morgan decided, his gaze remaining fixed on the doorway leading to the front hall long after she'd disappeared through it. Dressed like one, too, in sober, neutral colors designed along straight, concealing lines. The only piece missing from the picture was the sweet charity of soul one might reasonably expect in a woman of the cloth, but Jessica Simms was a vinegary bit of a thing whose habit of giving a nostril-pinching little sniff of suspicious disapproval around men spoke volumes.

Not that he necessarily held that against her. On the contrary, he applauded her for it. He'd seen enough tragedy resulting from people, particularly women and children, choosing to ignore their self-protective instincts where men were concerned.

Abruptly, he grabbed the empty wood basket and, with Shadow at his heels, strode through the mud room and out into the night, welcoming the sting of the still falling snow against his face, the bite of the wind funneling up from the valley. Anything to distract him from the memories too ready to leap out of his professional past—some of which would, he suspected, haunt him till the day he died.

It was Christmas, for Pete's sake—a time for families to come together in celebration. The trouble was, he'd seen too many ripped apart by violent crime and nothing he'd been able to do in the way of exacting justice had managed to heal them. Not chestnuts roasting, not plum puddings ablaze with rum, not children hanging stockings. Especially not children hanging stockings.

For a while, during the married years with Daphne, he'd hoped she'd become pregnant. He'd needed to know he could look after his own family, even if he couldn't always protect others'. He'd wanted his parents to know the joy of grandchildren. But the children hadn't come, Daphne hadn't stayed, and his parents had died within six months of each other.

So here he was, thirty-seven, with more money than he knew what to do with, a career that promised to elevate him to the Bench before he turned fifty, and spending another Christmas alone, except for Clancy and a woman he felt he should address as Sister!

Flinging enough wood into the basket to keep the stove well stoked until morning, he retraced his steps from the shed to the house. Already, the prints he'd made when he'd come out were powdered with a fresh layer of snow. It was going to be a classic white Christmas, the kind shown on nostalgic cards where women in fur muffs shepherded families to church and children gazed, wide-eyed, through square-paned windows draped in icicles.

Families, children.... Despite his best attempts to shut it out, the whole memory thing came full circle again, threatening to blanket him more thoroughly than the snow.

He shook his head impatiently. He should have stayed in Vancouver where it was probably raining, and those dim-witted ornamental cherry trees along the boulevards and seafronts were bursting with pale pink blossom in anticipation of a spring still three months away. Where he had friends who gathered in exclusive private clubs to nibble on Russian caviar and sip champagne. Where the women adjusted their sleek designer gowns and watched him with a certain hunger that, for a little while, he could return.

Instead, he was snowbound with the very proper Miss Simms who probably wouldn't know sexual appetite if it jumped up and bit her on the nose. Damn!

He kicked open the outside door and dumped the wood basket on the floor next to the tree Clancy had brought in at noon. On the other side of the wall, he could hear her puttering around the stove, opening the oven door, rattling cutlery.

She froze when he came into the kitchen, as if she'd suddenly come face to face with an intruder bent on unspeakable mischief. She stood on the far side of the table, knives and forks cradled in her graceful nun's hands, her big gray eyes all wide and startled, and it irritated the hell out of him.

"What's with the nervous tic?" he inquired.

She stared at him, the way a cornered kitten might. "Is it all right to do this?"

He frowned. "Do what?"

"Prepare the table for dinner."

"Of course it's all right," he snapped, his irritation boiling over. "Why on earth wouldn't it be?"

"It upset your hired hand, when he came in for lunch. He seemed to think I was interfering."

"Oh, that." Morgan selected a bottle of wine from the rack built next to the Welsh dresser and found a corkscrew. "It wasn't you so much as the memories you stirred up. Beyond making sure the plumbing doesn't freeze when I'm not here, he doesn't spend much time in the main house since his wife died. I guess coming in and seeing the place looking the way it did when she was alive took him aback, especially with it being so close to Christmas."

"I'm sorry. I had no idea."

"No reason you should." He took down two wine glasses. "Will you join me, or don't you drink?"

"A little red wine with dinner would be nice."

A little red wine with dinner would be nice, she said,

mouth all ready to pucker with disapproval. Oh, brother, it was going to be a long evening!

While she served the food, he filled the glasses and wondered unchivalrously if his getting roaring drunk might pass the time more pleasantly. She sat across from him and shook out her serviette, her movements refined, her manners impeccable, as if she'd been born with a silver spoon in her mouth and a flock of servants on hand to do her slightest bidding. And yet the meal she'd turned out suggested a more than passing familiarity with the working end of a kitchen.

They had cream soup made from carrots and flavoured with ginger, followed by stew with dumplings and rich brown gravy, and he had to admit the food went a good way toward improving his mood.

"These dumplings," he said, spearing one with his fork, "remind me of when Agnes, Clancy's wife, used to do the cooking. She always served them with venison, too."

"Venison?" Jessica Simms echoed, managing to turn rather pale even as she choked on her wine.

"Deer," he explained, thinking she hadn't understood.

She pressed her serviette hurriedly to her mouth and mumbled, "I was afraid that was what you meant."

"Why, what did you think you were eating?"

"Beef," she said faintly.

He laughed. "Same thing, more or less, except for the antlers."

"Oh!" She pushed aside her plate and forgot herself far enough to plant one elbow on the table as she covered her eyes with her hand.

"What's the matter, Jessica? You're obviously not a vegetarian, so it can't be that."

"It's the image that comes to mind when I think of deer."

"Does this happen every time you eat meat?" he inquired, trying to ignore how her hair gleamed in the lamplight. "Do you see little pigs dancing through the air when you fry bacon, or lambs cavorting when you—?"

"It's Rudolph," she said. "I see Rudolph…maybe because it's Christmas."

The red-nosed reindeer? Morgan leaned back in his chair, dumbstruck. "I'd never have figured you for the whimsical type," he finally admitted, smothering a grin. "Do you believe in Santa Claus, too?"

"No," she said, reverting to her usual prim self. "I learned a long time ago that he was the figment of other children's imaginations, but not mine. And I apologize for appearing to be such a fool. But I'm afraid that, much as I hate to see food going to waste, I simply cannot bring myself to eat…" she ventured another glance at the stew cooling on her plate and turned a shade paler "…that."

"Never mind," he said, oddly touched by this more susceptible side of her personality. "The dogs will love you for it. More to the point, though, is what can we find that you will eat?" He got up and opened the refrigerator door. "We've got eggs and ham and cheese. I could make us an omelette."

"Please don't trouble yourself," she said, the nun firmly in control again. "Please just go ahead with your meal before it gets cold."

"And what will you do?" he asked, irritation flaring up anew. "Huddle in the corner and subsist on bread and water?"

"I'll make a sandwich."

"You'll do no such thing." He grabbed the dogs' scrap bowl from the refrigerator and, picking up both plates, added their contents to what it already contained. "You've hardly slept in the last two days, it's hours since we ate lunch, and you're not going to bed on an empty stomach. I might be a lousy host, Jessica, but I'm not inhuman. We'll eat eggs—unless you see unhatched chickens…?''

"No." She got up and came to join him, spine erect, narrow hips swaying elegantly. "But I do insist on helping, since I'm putting you to so much trouble."

"For crying out loud, sit and enjoy your wine, and while I'm showing off my culinary skills keep me entertained by telling me why you didn't believe in Santa Claus when you were a kid."

"I grew up in a very…pragmatic household. My aunt didn't encourage fantasies, not even when my sister and I were very small."

He paused in the act of slicing the ham. "Aunt?"

"Selena and I were orphaned when we were kids, and were sent to live with my father's brother and his wife."

"And Auntie didn't much like being roped in as surrogate mother?"

"She was always very fair. She did her duty the best way she knew how, and so did my uncle."

Jeez! Morgan reached for an onion and began dicing it with uncommon violence. No wonder she was so bloody repressed. From the sound of it, where she'd grown up wasn't so far removed from a Victorian orphanage! "And debunking the myth of Santa Claus came under the heading of duty, did it? Does that mean you woke up to empty stockings on Christmas morning?"

"Oh, no." She took a dainty sip of wine. "We weren't in the least deprived materially. There was plenty of money and we always had lots of expensive gifts. They just didn't come wrapped in…magic."

He broke six eggs into a mixing bowl, added salt, a dash of pepper, a dollop of hot sauce, a pinch of dried parsley. "What about the tooth fairy?"

She smiled and it transformed her face, suffusing it with life and softening its pale angles with a warmth that left her almost pretty. "No tooth fairy, I'm afraid, just regular visits to the dentist and new toothbrushes every second month.''

''Well, I don't know....'' He whisked the eggs and threw a chunk of butter into the frying pan heating on the stove. ''It seems to me everyone deserves to start out with a little make-believe, a little magic. Special times to look back on, memories to treasure. Isn't that what childhood's all about?''

''We had special times.''

He poured the omelette over the sizzling butter and swirled the mixture around the edges of the pan, before tossing chopped onion and ham on top. ''Like what?'' he asked, adding a handful of grated cheese.

She sat and thought for a minute, her face a study in grave concentration again. ''I was given a leather-bound edition of the complete works of Shakespeare when I graduated from high school.''

''You must have been overwhelmed,'' he said dryly. ''Think of all that lewd material in the hands of an eighteen-year-old girl! It's a miracle you weren't seduced into a life of debauchery.''

She flung him a somewhat hunted look and in one gulp polished off half the wine remaining in her glass. ''I—''

He divided the omelette, flipped each portion onto the plates warming on the hearth, and waited for her to continue. When she showed no inclination to do so, he put her plate down in front of her and reached for the wine bottle. ''What were you going to say, Jessica?'' he asked, topping up both glasses.

''Nothing.''

The way her mouth clamped shut on the word had his internal radar picking up signals just as it did when he sensed a witness was about to commit perjury. Without knowing how, he'd stumbled on some aspect of her past which troubled her deeply but he knew he'd have to temper curiosity with patience if he wanted to discover what it was.

"In that case," he said casually, touching the rim of his glass to hers, "here's to another stab at dinner. *Bon appétit!*"

While he made short work of his share of the ome-lette, she pecked at hers like a nervous bird. Attempting to ease the tension a little, he said, "I meant to say earlier that the table looks very nice. It's usually clut-tered with stuff and I just clear a space big enough to accommodate my plate."

She dropped her fork with a clatter. "Oh, that reminds me, I found a stack of mail for you when I came in to get things ready for lunch and left it on the dresser, next to the clock. Let me get it for you, before I forget again."

He started to say, "There's no hurry," but she was already skittering out of her chair and scooping up a miscellany of mail-order catalogues and a handful of cards from the few people who knew he always spent Christmas at the ranch.

"Thanks," he said, when she dropped the bundle be-side his plate, and would have been happy to ignore it until tomorrow if his attention hadn't been caught by the return address on the topmost envelope.

Clarkville Penitentiary. The handwriting was unmis-takable, as neat and contained as the man who'd penned it. A jarring reminder that, no matter how much Morgan might like to fool himself, there was no escaping who he was. The real world had a way of following him, no matter where he went to hide.

He sensed her watching him. "Is there something wrong, Mr. Kincaid?"

"Apart from this 'Mr. Kincaid' business, no," he said shortly, tempted to toss the envelope in the stove unread. "Calling me Morgan won't compromise your virtue, you know."

"I suppose not."

"We have spent a night together, after all."

She flushed at that, the shocked, uptight pink of a virgin confronted by the nearest thing to original sin she'd ever seen. "But not in any familiar sense," she protested.

"No," he said, pushing away from the table. "Look, I don't mean to appear rude, but there's something here I should have attended to sooner and I'd prefer not to leave it any longer."

"Of course. I'm sorry if I've—"

"You haven't." Annoyed that she assumed his sudden restlessness was her fault and unwilling to explain that it was not, he brushed her apology aside and strode to the door. "I'm likely to be tied up on the phone for some time, so if you—"

"Please don't worry about me," she rushed to assure him. "I'll just finish my meal, then make an early night of it."

"In that case I'll see you in the morning." He nodded and left her to it. Once in the study with the door closed firmly behind him, he slit open the sealed envelope and withdrew the card inside.

A pen-and-ink drawing of Clarkville in winter stared up at him, its walls rising bleakly against the starkness of sky and countryside.

He flipped it open and read the contents inside. And knew at once that Clancy had been right. Crazy or not, Gabriel Parrish was bent on revenge. Other people might not recognize the threat hidden in the words "I owe you so much and hope to repay you very soon" but he did. He knew exactly what Gabriel Parrish was really saying.

Tapping the card against the surface of the desk, Morgan debated his options. They were pitifully few. He could run, which was really no option at all since running was not his style and would solve nothing, or he could go looking for his long-time enemy. Or he could wait for the enemy to come to him.

Briefly, he stared out at a night turned ghostly gray by the still falling snow and knew that of the three only the last made any sense. Which made getting rid of Jessica Simms a.s.a.p. all the more imperative.

CHAPTER FOUR

IT WAS late when Morgan came up to bed. Jessica had expected to be asleep long before then but had found her thoughts revolving around him too persistently for her to relax.

What a strange and moody man he was, charming and open one minute, brusque and reserved the next. She'd watched him in the kitchen, covertly taking stock of him as he whipped up the omelette. Had noticed his hands in particular, how finely shaped they were, how well cared for, with the nails short and scrupulously clean for all that he'd spent the afternoon in the stables.

Had noticed his long, strong legs, too, and remembered last night when they'd trapped hers and held her close to him. Not the sort of memory conducive to relaxation at all!

Then there'd been that other business at dinner. She'd felt like a fool for acting as she had when she'd discovered they were eating venison, and had expected another round of scorn from him. But although he'd laughed at her it had not been unkindly and she hadn't minded. In fact, she had been quite captivated by the way his wide, sexy mouth had curved with amusement.

His glance had met hers and he'd smiled at her over the rim of his glass. Behind him, the snow had swirled against the window, a chunk of wood in the stove had shifted and sent a shower of sparks up the chimney and, suddenly, it was Christmas and despite their being strangers a sort of intimacy had flared between them.

The kitchen had assumed a warmth that went beyond the heat from the fire, the wine had rolled more smoothly down her throat and taken with it the inhibitions behind which she hid so much of herself. She had felt safe; had known that, stranger or not, Morgan Kincaid was a man of integrity and that she had nothing to fear from him.

And then she'd brought up the subject of the mail and that had spoiled everything. He'd changed, become all dark and withdrawn, with a haunted sort of look about him as he'd weighed the one envelope on the palm of his hand.

Instinct had told her the sender was a woman who held the power to affect him, to move him, in a way that she, Jessica, had never enjoyed with a man.

The ambience had altered, become charged with tension, and she had felt herself again the interloper. The intimacy had shriveled, her habitual reserve had come slinking back, and she knew he had neither noticed nor cared that she regretted both.

It must have been close to midnight when his footsteps sounded on the stairs and light from the bathroom next door shone out into the night. Huddled beneath the down quilt, Jessica listened to the muffled tattoo of water running in the shower, and to her horror found visions of him standing there naked, with the water sluicing down his powerful body, springing alive in her mind's eye.

A surge of heat spiraled through her, disturbing, erotic. She remained in thrall to it even after the house sank into silence again; found herself wondering how it would have felt to be under that hot stream of water with him, with his hands gliding the length of her spine to define her buttocks, and his mouth fastening on hers, and his hard flesh fusing tightly within the dark, soft warmth of hers.

Appalled, she shot up in the bed, welcoming the chill slap of air against her bare shoulders. Such thoughts were unconscionable! She hadn't allowed herself such self-indulgent rubbish in over five years—not since Stuart McKinney had lied his way into her naive heart and seduced her pathetically grateful body.

Across the hall, a mattress creaked, a small sound in the overwhelming silence of the night, but enough to leave her brain feverish with yet another unpardonable image. Of Morgan Kincaid looming naked above her on the bed, of his hand pushing aside her silk nightgown to caress her naked breast, of his knee nudging apart her thighs.

The blood roared in her ears, scorching, shameful. What was the matter with her? Jessica Simms, headmistress of the Springhill Island Private School for Girls, was famous for the absolute incorruptibility of her morals. What would her board of governors have to say if they could see her now, at the mercy of a sexual fantasy so powerful that she was practically writhing with arousal—and all over a man she'd met only twenty-four hours before and about whom she knew nothing but his name?

Flinging aside the feather duvet, she swung her feet to the smooth pine floor. Not a crack of light showed anywhere as she sneaked down the hall and into the bathroom, with her nightgown whispering around her ankles.

Once inside, she locked the door and crossed to the hand-painted wash basin. Her eyes, when she glanced in the gilt-framed mirror hanging on the wall, stared back at her, their focus glazed.

Aghast all over again, she repeatedly dashed cold water over her face and neck, attempting to chase away with pure discomfort what she couldn't dislodge with logic or propriety. Only when the flush had died from her skin and her pulse approached its normal steady rate did she turn off the flow of water, replace the towel on the brass rail, and let herself out of the bathroom.

He was waiting for her outside in the hall, illuminated by a beam of light spilling from his room. He wore a knee-length navy terry-cloth robe which was tied loosely at the waist, and showed a great deal of strong masculine chest from the top and equally strong, masculine calves from the bottom. Try though she might, Jessica couldn't stop herself from staring.

"Hey," he said, his husky voice washing over her, drifting over her bare shoulders and down between her breasts, "are you sick or something?"

Was she? Had she been infected by some strange virus, and did that account for her unmanageable state of mind? "I was thirsty," she mumbled, refusing to meet his glance.

"You look flushed, as if you might be coming down with something." He flung out one hand in a gesture of unmistakable resentment. "Hell, that's the last thing I need."

"I am not ill," Jessica said firmly.

"It wouldn't surprise me if you were," he said, taking in the thin straps that held up the flimsy fabric of her nightgown. "Don't you own *any* decent winter clothing?"

"If by that you mean flannelette pyjamas, no." She threw a glance at him and without considering the wisdom of her words added, "And you're a fine one to talk. I haven't seen so much exposed skin on a man since dear knows when!"

He looked down and gave the terry-cloth robe a twitch to make sure he was decent, a move that left her wondering if he was stark naked underneath.

He knew, as surely as if she'd voiced her curiosity aloud. "Don't hold your breath, Miss Simms," he drawled. "You've seen all I intend to show."

Evil creature! How could she ever have thought him attractive?

Jessica snapped her jaws together and swung away, intending to put the solid wood of her bedroom door between him and her quickly, before her composure crumbled completely. She hadn't gone two steps, however, when, with the eerie sound of a ghost keening to be free, a mournful howl filled the house, its source so close that it seemed to emanate from the very wall in front of her.

Seasoned students at the school were fond of tormenting homesick newcomers with tales of spooks haunting the halls of the junior dormitory. Pragmatist that she was, Jessica always successfully nipped such ideas in the bud, but, just then, just for a moment, her grip on reality slipped and left her at the mercy of the most bizarre foolishness. Just for as long as it took her to spring back with a startled gasp and come up against Morgan Kincaid's solid, underclothed frame.

At that, *everything* fled her mind except for the fact that, all at once, she was on the brink of realizing her earlier fantasy. She could feel the sculpted muscle of his chest at her shoulder blades, his hand in the small of her back, his breath flowing warmly over the nape of her neck.

But the sad fact was, it was not magical at all.

He didn't pull her protectively close, he moved her away with ill-concealed exasperation. "For crying out loud, it's just the wind in the chimney," he said, his voice about as chill as the night outside. "It means the weather's swung around and is blowing in from the north-east again and that we're in for another storm."

"Really." She tugged the straps of her nightgown firmly into place and, with a haughty little toss of her head meant to intimate that she'd found the physical contact every bit as disagreeable as he had, increased the distance between him and her. "Well, I certainly hope that won't delay my departure tomorrow."

"So do I," he muttered on a heartfelt sigh, before he disappeared into his room. "So do I!"

* * *

The next morning, Jessica awoke to find her room flooded with reflected brilliance and the sort of hush that cushioned a world buried in snow. Drifts lay halfway up the window and any trace of a road up to the house had been completely obliterated. Above the trees a pewter sky promised more of the same punishment, although the wind appeared to have died. She didn't need anyone to tell her she wouldn't be going anywhere today.

Morgan Kincaid had left a note propped up on the kitchen table. "Gone out to take care of the animals. Help yourself to breakfast and keep the fire and coffee pot going. Be back in a couple of hours."

It was barely nine o'clock. Jessica discovered that the coffee in the pot too closely resembled used motor oil to warrant human consumption and, while she waited for a fresh pot to brew, took a mandarin orange from the bowl on the Welsh dresser and went on a tour of the rest of the main floor of the house.

In light of the rather spartan decor in the bedrooms, she didn't expect too much and was pleasantly surprised to find, to the right of the stairs, a living room some twenty-five feet long by about fifteen feet wide, furnished in faded rose damask.

A massive stone-faced fireplace flanked by built-in bookcases occupied center place on the east wall. Leaded windows looked out on the valley to the south and the steep hill leading up to the cliffs to the north. Painted molding crowned the walls and framed the glass doors leading to a formal dining room.

Clearly, however, neither room had been used in quite some time. The air was flat and stale. A film of dust covered the occasional tables and the top of the old-fashioned pump organ under the south windows in the living room.

Although the hearth had been swept clean, a spider had woven an intricate pattern across one corner of the chimney opening and cobwebs swayed from the silk shades of various lamps.

In some ways, the dining room had fared no better. Crystal stemware dulled by dust waited at one end of the table. The hearth contained the dead ashes of a fire and drippings of wax had overflowed the tarnished silver candelabra to pool on the fine oak sideboard, as though dinner guests either had upped and left before the start of the meal or simply not shown up at all.

A terrible waste, Jessica thought, popping the last segment of mandarin orange in her mouth and retracing her steps. Rooms like these ought to be used instead of being left to molder. If she were mistress of this house, she'd have flowering plants on the mantelpiece, on the carved walnut chest behind the sofa, on top of the organ and in the middle of the dining table. Scarlet poinsettias, snowy cyclamen, rosy pink azaleas. And sprigs of holly tucked into graceful swags of evergreen over the doorway and windows.

The muffled tramp of boots on the back porch alerted her to Morgan Kincaid's return. By the time she'd made her way back to the kitchen, he and Clancy Roper had helped themselves to the better part of the fresh pot of coffee and were warming their backsides at the stove.

"Good afternoon," Morgan declared sunnily, glancing pointedly at the clock which showed twenty past nine.

Jessica supposed he was trying to be funny and had to admit she was relieved. In view of his parting words the night before, humor, however feeble, was the last thing she expected from him.

"It's not quite that late, surely?" she said, and wished she didn't always have to sound so much like a schoolmarm.

"Day's half over," Clancy Roper informed her, depleting the coffee supply again. "If we slept in till all hours like you, woman, nothing'd ever get done right around here."

He was as difficult an individual as Morgan Kincaid,

without the latter's good looks or unexpected bursts of charm to redeem him. "I dare say if I lived here and had chores to do I'd have to agree with you," she said. "But since I don't your point is scarcely relevant, is it?"

"Long as you're here, you've got chores." He jerked his head at the window. "See that sky out there? Loaded, it is. With snow," he added, as if she were too mentally defective to be able to figure out the simplest facts for herself. "And it'll be coming down before much longer. We ain't got time to be fixin' meals, missy, nor keeping fires goin'. We got work to do. Men's work."

Morgan Kincaid filled another mug with what was left of the coffee and handed it to her with a smile. "What Clancy's trying to tell you, in his uniquely subtle way, is that taking care of the horses is our first priority so…"

That smile undid her, seducing her so potently that she'd probably have gone out in her flimsy boots and unsuitable clothes and mucked out the stables for him if he'd asked her to. "So you'd like me to take over in here," she finished for him.

His smile deepened to reveal dimples of all things, one on each side of his mouth. "We'd appreciate it, Jessica." He glanced regretfully at the lowering sky beyond the window. "Especially since there's no way I can get you out of here today. The road is impassable, as I'm sure you must realize."

"I understand that." She shrugged her acceptance of what was patently obvious to the most untutored eye. "But I'd like to phone the hospital and let my sister know."

"Can't. All the lines are down," Clancy said, with manifest satisfaction at seeing her thwarted yet again. "If it weren't for the emergency generator, you'd be trimming oil lamps come sunset."

Morgan shot her a commiserating look. "He's right. I wish I could tell you the line crew will be out to fix the phone before tonight but it's more likely to be several days.''

"Surely it's only a matter of joining together a few wires. Isn't that something you could do?''

"If I knew where to start looking, yes, probably. But we're talking about ten miles or more of line, Jessica, and if I could follow that I could just as easily get you down to the main highway.''

"Reckon we've got ourselves a housekeeper over Christmas, Morgan.'' Clancy cackled with malicious delight. "Know how to pluck and dress a turkey, woman?''

"No,'' Jessica snapped. "So unless you do, Mr. Roper, it'll be cheese sandwiches for dinner on Christmas Day.''

Stifling a grin, Morgan said, "Quit needling her, Clancy, and count your blessings.''

Jessica stared at him. *"Count your blessings?"* she echoed. "Last night, the only blessing you were hoping for was my speedy exit from your life. Would you mind telling me what's happened—apart from a devastating snow storm—to bring on this burst of seasonal goodwill?''

He and Clancy Roper exchanged glances loaded with mysterious significance. Finally, he said smoothly, "You're not the only one inconvenienced by the weather. The Wrights, a couple from the other side of Sentinel Pass, come up here three times a week as a rule. Ted lends a hand around the stables and Betty does a bit of housekeeping.''

A very little bit, Jessica concluded, considering what she'd so far observed about the house. At best, the woman swiped a damp cloth over the most visible spots, but clearly didn't exert herself to do a more thorough cleaning.

"Obviously they're not going to make it up here today, any more than you're going to get to Whistling

Valley." Morgan said. "I know you're worried about your sister, but you said yourself she's in good hands and doing well."

He stopped and smiled again, more winningly than ever, then went on persuasively, "So if you're willing to take over in the house—?"

"And what if I break some hallowed tradition?" Jessica cut in. "Or touch something sacred?"

Furiously, Clancy banged his coffee cup down on the table, slopping its contents all over everything. "See what you've gone and started, Morgan?"

Another glance passed between the two men, then Morgan said, "Let it go, pal. We can afford to relax for the next couple of days."

Clancy seemed tempted to argue but something in Morgan's expression deterred him. "As you say," he muttered sullenly. "At least she knows how to cook."

"So," Morgan said, swinging his glance back to Jessica, "what about it? We might as well all try to get along."

"True." Jessica looked around the kitchen, at Clancy's moldy old felt stetson parked on the table and dripping melted snow among the remains of the breakfast dishes, at the bacon grease congealing in the frying pan on the counter next to the sink. "But if you think I'm going to be a lackey to your slovenly habits for the next couple of days, think again."

She flung out her hand in a gesture of disgust that encompassed the entire kitchen. "I'm not used to living in a pig sty, and I refuse to do so when there's no need."

"As long as there's livestock needs tendin' to," Clancy said, "dishes sittin' in the sink ain't exactly a priority."

"I appreciate that and I'm more than happy to pull my weight around the house, but you..." Jessica fixed him with the same determined look she afforded difficult students "...you will mend your ways and show a little appreciation. I will clean and cook and do my best to bring a little Christmas spirit into this house, but I cannot—and will not—do it alone.''

Morgan looked uneasy. ''Exactly what is it you'd like us to do?''

''Well, for a start, I see no reason for us to be falling all over one another in the kitchen when there's a perfectly lovely room going to waste down the hall. Two rooms, in fact, and neither looks as if anyone's set foot in it in months. So when you come in for lunch I'd like you to light fires in the hearths to take the chill out of the air, and I'll serve the evening meal in the dining room.''

''I gather you've taken a grand tour of the main floor,'' Morgan observed dryly.

''Hah!'' Clancy crowed. ''Snoopin's what she's been doin', Morgan. Didn't I tell you she would?''

''And you'll dress for dinner,'' Jessica went on, unfazed by the interruptions, ''in something other than the blue jeans you've apparently been sleeping in for the last week, Mr. Roper. It is almost Christmas, after all.''

''Dress for dinner because it's Christmas?'' Clancy practically spluttered with rage. ''Confound it, woman, I'm not—''

She planted her fists on her hips. ''Scrooge said more or less the same thing much more eloquently a long time ago, Mr. Roper, so spare me your version of the old 'Bah, humbug'. It's my way or bread and cheese. Take it or leave it.''

''We'll take it,'' Morgan said hurriedly. ''After lunch, we'll set up the tree in the living room and you can go to it. Make the place as festive as you like and we'll put on our party manners. Now grab your hat, Clancy, and let's get that mare settled before we have to dig our way from here to the stables.''

He was almost out of the door when he suddenly

turned back. "Oh, and by the way, stay inside the house, Jessica. It's safer."

"Safer?" What an odd choice of word. "Safer how?"

He paused fractionally and if she hadn't already learned from experience that he was one of the most forthright men she'd ever met she'd have thought he was concocting a lie. "You could get frostbite," he said. "In this weather it can happen in a matter of minutes, especially to someone dressed so inadequately."

Honestly, she thought, watching from the window above the sink as the men and dogs made their way back to the stables, the way Morgan acted at times, one would have thought he had next-door neighbors watching from behind starched lace curtains and jumping to all the wrong conclusions about the woman he'd brought into his home.

As for his obsession with the weather and her clothes, it bordered on preposterous.

"You'll be digging yourself out of more than snow at this rate," Clancy predicted gloomily as they bent into the wind and slogged toward the stables. "I'm tellin' you, Morgan, you keep givin' in to that woman and findin' reasons not to get rid of her, and before you know it you'll be up to your neck in more trouble than even you can handle."

Morgan squinted at the sky. "It's out of my hands, at least for the time being. You don't need me to tell you there's no way to send her on her way until the weather lets up. For now, she's as safe here as anywhere."

"T'ain't just her safety I'm worryin' about, Morgan, it's yours as well. You get a certain hungry look about you whenever you clap eyes on her and it gives me the willies. Ain't you learned your lesson yet where fancy city women are concerned? Heck, if she thinks the way you live up here ain't squeaky clean, what do you reckon she'd have to say about the muck you deal with down in the city? Well, I'll tell you," Clancy continued, barely stopping to draw breath. "She'd take a hike, just like the other one did, and what's that gonna leave you with, Morgan, apart from a cartload of heartache you don't need?"

"Not that I don't appreciate your concern, old friend," Morgan remarked, "but in this case it's misdirected. I've already told you, Jessica Simms is no more my type than she's yours and it'll be a cold day in hell before I get myself hooked up with someone like her."

They were fine words, uttered with enough conviction to silence Clancy, and Morgan might have believed them himself if he hadn't suddenly remembered how she'd looked on the landing the night before. Who'd have expected she'd favor silk nightwear so translucent that if the light had been shining from behind her, instead of in front, there'd be little left to his imagination regarding her surprisingly elegant, fine-boned body?

As for his physical response at finding her suddenly pressed up against him, *that* didn't mean a damned thing beyond the fact that he functioned exactly as any normal man would under the circumstances. Of far greater import was his knowledge that the circumstances were not all that they seemed. Fraught with potential danger, they were about as far from normal as they could get, and that was something he couldn't afford to forget.

Clancy surveyed him quietly for a moment then switched to the subject that was really preying on their minds. "How far you reckon Parrish'll get before they catch him?"

"Depends how much ground he covered before the weather set in." Morgan glanced up at the sky. "Wherever he is now is where he'll be staying until things let up."

"Could be he'll freeze to death and save us all a load of trouble."

"Unlikely. Parrish is no fool, Clancy, and it would be

a mistake to underestimate him. I made a couple of calls last night and from what I gathered his was no spur-of-the-moment run for freedom; it was something he'd planned to the last detail. You can be sure he'd have taken all eventualities into account, including the weather."

Morgan slid back the heavy stable door and followed Clancy inside, swatting snow from the brim of his stetson. "The point is, he's nowhere near here or we'd know about it by now. Which means that as long as we keep an ear out for the news—and I'm counting on you there, Clancy; I don't want her picking up on anything that might come across on the kitchen radio—we can afford to relax and enjoy the next few days."

He cast a stealthy glance at his stable hand and chose his next words carefully. "It also means we can be a bit more hospitable to our house guest. No point in arousing her suspicions any more than we already have, nor in causing her more anxiety than she's already got."

"Could be you're right. Don't fancy having a hysterical woman on our hands should things suddenly go sour."

"Exactly. And weren't you the one, yesterday, reminiscing about a woman's touch at Christmas, and how it used to be when Agnes was still alive?"

Clancy reared up like the stallion that had broken his thigh ten years before and left one of his legs permanently shorter than the other. "Jessica Simms ain't Agnes!"

"But she can cook and clean, pal, and if this blizzard keeps up, knowing the house is warm and that dinner's waiting on the table won't be such a bad thing."

"She still ain't Agnes." Clancy flung the statement over his shoulder, resentment rife in the crooked line of his spine.

Tamping down on the sharp reply begging for air space, Morgan tossed a fresh bale of hay into the nearest manger. Was Clancy getting more obstreperous with age, or was it that his own nerves were more on edge than he cared to admit?

"What do you want me to say? That we'll gang up on Jessica Simms, just to keep ourselves in shape in case Gabriel Parrish shows up? Because if so you're going to be disappointed. It's almost Christmas Eve, for Pete's sake, and I just don't have any appetite for waging unnecessary war for the next couple of days. Because, with the best will in the world, the road crews are going to take at least that long to make it up here—"

"Don't need to wait on no road crews," Clancy informed him morosely. "You got a perfectly good snowmobile in the garage and could have that woman out of here in less than an hour, if you had a mind to."

"And do what with her?" Morgan snapped. "Leave her stranded at Stedman's service station? Use your head, Clancy! Even if her car's fixed, she won't be driving anywhere until the highway's made passable again; nor will anyone else. Can't you make the best of what's just as lousy a situation for her as it is for us, or will it give you greater satisfaction to have us all at each other's throats?"

"Lordy, Morgan Kincaid, you ain't been this twitchy since your wife upped and left." Clancy slewed a crafty glance his way. "Don't like to think what that might mean."

"Then quit thinking at all! That way you'll jump to fewer wrong conclusions. A lot of people will tell you I can be a real bastard to deal with at times, and they're right, especially when it comes to my work, but I'm damned if I'm going out of my way to be unpleasant just to satisfy you. If you can't extend a bit of Christmas cheer to a stranger, Clancy, you're welcome to hole up in your own quarters until the weather breaks and Jessica's out of here."

"You ain't spoke to me in that tone in over three

years, Morgan,'' Clancy complained again. ''Not since your ex took you to the cleaners in the divorce court then ran off to Mexico with her lover.''

Like a dentist's drill coming too close to a nerve, Clancy's last remark needled home. Morgan braced himself and grew very still, a bad sign to those who knew him in a professional context.

Clancy knew it, too. He sucked in a long-suffering breath and muttered, ''But you're the boss. If makin' nice is what you're suddenly payin' me for, makin' nice is what you'll get.'' He swung around and started for the mare's stall at the far end of the stable, his limp more pronounced than usual as though to underline his resentment. ''Not that I got to like it any. No, sir, I ain't got to like it one little bit.''

CHAPTER FIVE

JESSICA took steaks from the freezer and left them to thaw for dinner, prepared ham and mushroom stuffed potatoes for lunch, then spent the remainder of the morning cleaning the house. A couple of hours of straight elbow grease effected a transformation that was only a little less amazing than the utter satisfaction she experienced as she polished and mopped.

Not that she was inept in such a role. Far from it, as the results of her efforts soon showed. But the lifestyle she'd chosen for herself, solitary and painstakingly professional, didn't call for much in the way of domesticity.

A sense of home and hearth had been a luxury others had denied her as a child and from which necessity had distanced her as an adult. Her residence at the school was entirely self-contained, an austerely elegant little house set in a private section of the grounds, but she spent little time there. In addition to her administrative duties, the endless round of board meetings and other related fund-raising events intruded too frequently to allow for that.

Here, though, she was free to play at what other women took for granted as a routine part of daily life. For however long the weather held her captive, she could create the sort of ambience that had no place in her real life. She could hum carols as she worked, raid the preserves in the pantry and make mince tarts, and plan menus for the next two days.

And she did. With a vengeance. When the men and dogs showed up shortly after noon, the air was filled with the inviting aroma of hot mincemeat tarts subtly underscored by furniture wax and pine-scented floor cleaner.

Morgan and Clancy left their hats and boots in the mud room and she knew that they noticed how the kitchen sparkled from the way they sat gingerly at the gleaming table and sort of examined everything from under lowered brows, but there were no snide comments.

There was no conversation at all, in fact, unless the grunt issuing from Clancy Roper's tight-lipped mouth was to be taken as appreciation of the food he apparently enjoyed, if the speed with which he wolfed it down was any indication. Instead, a miasma of hostility hung heavily between the two men, creating an even more pervasive and disquieting chill than the weather.

Even the dogs picked up on it, slinking under the table and remaining there throughout the meal. The atmosphere was about as cheery as a wake and so thoroughly destroyed the ambience she had worked hard to create that Jessica couldn't keep quiet.

Atypically, she was spoiling for a fight, in part because Clancy put her back up in the way that he sniffed his disapproval of her, and in part to prove to herself that she wasn't in thrall to some misplaced sexual fantasy where Morgan Kincaid was concerned.

It was, she reasoned, impossible to entertain erotic dreams about a man she found thoroughly obnoxious.

"Not that I expect either of you to go overboard with compliments or anything," she said tersely as the last mince tart disappeared and both men pushed back their chairs, prepared to leave the table as taciturnly as they'd sat down, "but a simple 'thank you' would be appreciated. Or is it that, in filling your stomachs with good hot food, you consider I'm merely serving the purpose for which God intended me?"

"I seldom waste time trying to second-guess the Almighty, particularly when it comes to women," Morgan replied with equal brevity.

As if members of the female sex in general and she in particular were an anomaly sent to try the patience of reasonable men! "Very broad-minded of you, I'm sure," she spat. "And what time would you like me to serve dinner, master?"

Clancy snickered and Morgan said testily, "For crying out loud, stop acting as if you're the scullery maid! I thought it was mutually agreed that you'd take care of things on the home front so that we could get through the outside work in reasonable time, but if you think your talents would be better employed in the stables all you have to do is say so."

"Well...no." Jessica had the grace to look embarrassed. "I don't know much about horses and I really don't mind holding the fort in here."

"We appreciate that—and the good food. Don't we, Clancy?"

Clancy inclined his head a fraction and shuffled his stockinged feet. "If you say so."

Morgan sighed in a way that suggested he was shouldering more troubles than Jessica could begin to understand, then spread his hands in appeal. "I know this isn't the sort of Christmas either of you had in mind, and it isn't exactly my idea of a picnic in the park either, but we're stuck with it and each other. Can we please just try to make the best of it?"

"Yes," Jessica said in a small voice. It wasn't like her to be so temperamental. But then, nothing about her behavior had been quite normal since she'd met Morgan Kincaid.

"Okay. It starts to get dark about four, by which time we'll be done with the animals, so why don't we plan to eat around seven? That'll give us time to clean up a bit and do justice to your cooking. We might even go so far as to enjoy a drink before dinner." He swung another glance at his stable hand that was little short of a challenge. "Right?"

Clancy pasted an ingratiating smile on his weathered old face. "Whatever you say, boss."

Morgan's response was edged with steel. "Glad you've decided to see things my way."

"Anythin' else, Mr. Kincaid, sir, before I get back to what I'm bein' paid to do?"

"Not a damn thing." The reply gusted out on a breath of exasperation. "I'll join you shortly, although if something comes up and you need me sooner you know where to find me."

Clancy spared Jessica a direct glare for the first time since he'd come in for lunch. "You bet. Ain't no doubt at all in my mind about where *you'll* be."

"Now what have I done to upset him?" she asked, when the door had slammed shut behind him and Ben.

"More than usual, you mean?" Morgan ran a weary hand through his hair.

Jessica stared at him in surprise. "You're surely not saying he's always this...?"

"Cantankerous?" He let out a bark of a laugh. "Not as a rule, no. Maybe it's just the season. Not everyone likes to make a big deal of Christmas."

But she didn't believe him. The tree had been cut and ready to bring into the house when she'd shown up on the scene. "There's more to it than that. He bitterly resents your letting me stay here, doesn't he? And not just because I happened to bring out his wife's best table linen."

Morgan flexed his shoulders and, hooking his thumbs on his hips, pressed the fingers of each hand to the small of his back. "Don't take offense, Jessica. It's not you personally."

She angled a wry look his way. "I see. He just hates people in general."

At her sarcasm, the suggestion of a grin lightened Morgan's expression. "He leads a pretty solitary life. Goes for weeks sometimes with no company other than the dogs and the horses, except for those days when the Wrights are here. That can be hard on a man's party manners, especially if he suddenly finds himself thrust into the company of a woman.''

''I don't buy that for a minute!'' She scooped up the dirty dishes, piled them in the sink, and began rinsing them. ''For heaven's sake, Morgan, I'm a visitor who'll be gone in a matter of days and who's trying to earn her keep in the meantime, not a permanent threat to his lifestyle.''

''I know.''

''Not only that, he was married at one time and I assume from the way he reacted to my touching her things that he holds his wife's memory sacred and that theirs was a long and happy marriage.''

A grimace passed over his face then, a strange, bitter expression that ironed Morgan's mouth into an unsmiling seam. ''That's because he was smart enough to choose a woman who loved him enough to accept him for what he was and never tried to change him.''

So that was it! The suspicion she'd entertained last night, that there was a woman in Morgan Kincaid's life, sharpened to near certainty. His inexplicable shifts of mood, the sudden edge in his voice complemented by a glacial sheen in his eyes found their origin in a marriage gone sour. If she'd guessed right, the question was, how significant a role did the absent wife presently enjoy?

Jessica itched to know and refused to ask. His matrimonial affairs were no more her business than her single status was his. Except that if a wife *was* lurking in the background, and Jessica could know that for certain, it would be enough to kill her lingering attraction to him. She might be all sorts of a fool where men were concerned, but she wasn't idiot enough to repeat past mistakes.

''Something wrong, Jessica?''

''No.'' She shook her head, as much to dislodge her

thoughts as to answer him. "Shouldn't you be getting back outside to help Clancy?"

"I can spare a few minutes to help you out in here first."

"I can manage on my own," she said hastily, more aware than ever that she was afraid to be alone with him. Afraid that the unholy thoughts she'd entertained the night before would return in full force and that, this time, she wouldn't so easily be able to hide their effect on her.

Even now, she was thoroughly aware of him as he leaned against the edge of the counter and watched her doing the dishes. He had such long legs, such trim hips. He was trim all over, she thought, inspecting him slyly, but with the leanly muscled build of a man who worked off the frustrations of daily life in a gym or on a squash court rather than around horses. In fact, he neither spoke nor looked like her idea of a rancher. But then, most of what she knew she'd learned from movies.

Picking up a dish towel, he began drying the cutlery she'd stacked on the draining board. "No need to tackle it alone when an extra pair of hands will cut the job in half," he said.

"I like to keep busy," she replied, disturbingly aware of his shoulder mere inches from hers, of his elbow brushing her arm as he reached for the soup spoons.

"And you will, if you're serious about our using the other rooms over the holiday. I don't think they've seen the working end of a dust rag in the better part of a year."

"Shame on you," she said lightly, concentrating on the dishes in the sink, which were a much safer subject than his physique. "You should make your regular housekeeper earn her money."

He finished drying the last of the cutlery and flung down the dish towel. "You've rinsed those plates to within an inch of their lives," he chided her, tucking the tail of his shirt into the narrow waist of his blue jeans.

"If you're determined you're not going to let me help you finish them, then leave them to drip dry and let's get out of this kitchen."

"You mean I'm allowed to put my feet up for half an hour?"

"Hell, no." He grinned at her, suddenly seeming younger and more carefree than he had at any time since he'd found her in the avalanche shed. "We're going to light those fires you were asking for, and bring in the Christmas tree. Then I'm going to get my hide outside before Clancy nails it to the wall, and you're going to get busy turning this place into a Dickensian Christmas card."

But although the fires started easily enough the tree wasn't quite so cooperative. Despite Morgan's best efforts, it wouldn't stand straight in the big brass planter he hauled in from his office. In the end, Jessica had to support the trunk while he jammed pieces of firewood around the base to hold it firmly in place, and by the time that was accomplished she had pine needles in her hair and down her neck, another half hour had passed, and he was swearing fluently.

"Damned thing!" he muttered, finally crawling out from under the lower boughs. "Why couldn't Clancy have cut something smaller?"

But Jessica, stepping back to take in the general effect, was overawed by the graceful symmetry of the branches and the way the top of the tree almost brushed the high ceiling. "It's perfect!" she breathed. "Morgan, it's the most beautiful Christmas tree I've ever seen."

He grimaced at the pine sap staining his hands. "I find that hard to believe. You don't strike me as the type who'd ever settle for anything less than perfection."

"That just goes to show how little you know about me," she said, recalling the sterile silver foil imitation of the real thing that had been Aunt Edith's idea of Christmas decor. "Tacky clichés aren't my style, dear," she'd sneered, the one year Jessica had dared ask for the kind of traditional tree she remembered from the days when her parents were alive.

"True." Morgan gave the trunk a last nudge to make sure it was standing firm. "We are, as you've already pointed out, virtual strangers, yet here we are playing house together, so don't you think it's time we got to know each other a little better?"

Playing house. That was it exactly. They'd been forced into taking part in a charade, but none of it was real. In a few days she'd be on her way, their separate lives would pick up where they'd left off, and a week from now he'd have erased her from memory. The tree would be tossed outside and discarded, its purpose served. And she would never see this place or him again.

Jessica found the thought profoundly depressing.

"Aren't you going to gratify my curiosity?"

Realizing that he was observing her closely, she sought to distract him by plucking at a strand of dead grass clinging to a lower limb of the tree. "I thought you were in a hurry to get back to the stables."

He watched her a moment longer, then said, "You're right. The story of your life will have to wait until later."

Fascinate him with tales of her hopeless inability to inspire others to love her as they always so easily loved her sister? Hardly!

"The story of my life," she told him firmly, "isn't exactly the kind of thing that makes for riveting dinner conversation."

Unexpectedly, he reached out and smoothed his hand over her hair, removing several stray pine needles as he did so. "Let me be the judge of that."

The contact, though brief, was electrifying. She had a sudden insane urge to imprison his hand against her face, to turn her head and press her mouth to his resin-stained palm. Instead, she shook herself free of him.

He smiled down at her, easy and relaxed in contrast

to the stifling tension gripping her. "You look as if you've been dragged through a hedge backwards. Are you sure you can handle trimming this monster by yourself? It's nearly ten feet tall, you know."

"Provide me with decorations and a stepladder, and I'll manage."

She always managed—to repress the craving for love that so easily backfired and ended up hurting her, to hide her fear of rejection, to project an air of cool independence. These were the parameters within which she lived and she would do well to remember that, instead of straying beyond them to weave dangerous romantic fantasies around Morgan Kincaid.

"A stepladder I have," he said, "and you'll find plenty of decorations in the storage closet under the stairs, though I should warn you that they'll take some sorting out. Clancy and I just jammed everything into boxes last year without regard for any sort of order. It was the first Christmas after Agnes's death and post-holiday depression struck pretty hard."

He hadn't exaggerated. It took her the rest of the afternoon to untangle the lengths of colored lights she found in the first box, and check for burned-out bulbs. Finally satisfied that they were all working, she pulled the stepladder close to the tree and began threading the lights through the branches, becoming so absorbed in the task that she barely noticed the afternoon slipping away.

All her concentration was focused on bringing the tree to light and life before the men came back; to have made a start on creating that Dickensian Christmas card Morgan had talked about.

They finished in the stables earlier than Morgan had expected, mostly because Clancy was still sulking and refused to be drawn into conversation. It had started to snow again, bitter, persistent little flakes that stung Morgan's face as he tramped back to the house at about a quarter to four.

There was no sound of activity when he let himself in the back door, no sign of dinner being prepared, and he wondered, with a stab of dismay, if she'd been foolhardy enough to ignore his warning about remaining safely indoors.

Moving on silent feet down the hall, he placed the flat of his hand against the living-room door and nudged it ajar. "Jessica?"

He heard her gasp of alarm, saw the swirl of her skirt and a brief flash of thigh as she teetered atop the stepladder, and was across the room in an instant. "Steady," he murmured, reaching up to anchor her at her waist.

She swayed beneath his touch, and said breathlessly, "Oh, you startled me!"

"Sorry," he said, despising the weakness that made him want to slide his hands over her hips and down the elegant length of her legs. Until that moment, he had not realized how long and shapely they were. "I thought you'd be done by now."

"Heavens, no! I've only just finished stringing lights." She stretched up to secure the illuminated silver star that belonged on the top of the tree, and he instinctively tightened his hold on her, this time aware of how tiny her waist was, how delicately rounded her hips. "There, that should do it."

"Let's turn them on, then, and see how they look." He turned away as she stepped daintily down the ladder and wondered just how it had come about that he no longer saw her as a nun-like creature beyond the pale of a man's unruly appetite.

Dismayed more than he cared to admit by the conflicting emotions she aroused in him, he bent down to plug the electric cord into a nearby outlet and heard her exhalation of pleasure as the room filled with soft light.

"Oh," she sighed, clasping her hands under her chin in pure delight. "Oh, Morgan, look! It's magical!"

But he looked at her instead, and what he saw on her face left him speechless. She looked radiant and innocent and young and beautiful and nothing at all like the severe, uptight woman he'd so reluctantly accepted into his home a mere twenty-four hours before.

The lights shimmered in the gleam of her hair, in the depths of her eyes, and painted alluring shadows beneath her cheekbones and down her throat. The plain navy skirt hung in graceful folds about her calves and the tailored white blouse, stained with rainbow reflections from the tree, molded itself to her with an intimacy that left him sour with envy.

"You look pretty magical yourself, Jessica Simms," he said thickly, his gaze clinging to hers.

It was as well that the back door thumped open just then or he might have made the colossal mistake of touching her. As it was, there came the slither of wet paws down the hall and the next minute Shadow tore into the room, tongue lolling and tail threatening terrible damage to the tree.

"I guess I should start thinking about dinner," Jessica said, laughingly fending off the exuberant dog.

Morgan cornered the retriever and grabbed her by the collar. "Why don't I take over kitchen duty tonight," he suggested, "and leave you to finish what you started in here? It would be nice to have the tree—as well as us—all dressed up for dinner."

"Your taking over kitchen duty isn't part of our deal."

Nor was finding himself embarrassingly aroused by her proximity! "I'll make an exception just this once— unless you're willing to settle for eating at the kitchen table again."

"No." She spun away from him and surveyed her handiwork thus far. "It won't take me long to finish the

tree now, so..." the lights struck a garish note beside
the uncertain sweetness of the smile she angled at him
over her shoulder "...if you're sure you don't mind taking care of dinner that'll leave me enough time to finish
cleaning the dining room."

"It's a deal," he said, and seized the chance to put
the length of the house between them before he made a
complete fool of himself.

The decorations were an odd mix. One carton contained
a glossy assortment of electric-blue glass balls that
shrieked designer choice, another held an artificial tree
done up to look like a snow-encrusted fir.

But then she found another box on another shelf con-
taining treasures that went back fifty years or more. Delicate spun-glass ornaments spangled with stars, cranberry velvet bows sewn with tiny seed-pearls,
hand-crocheted snowflakes so light and fine they'd drift
in the air just like the real thing. And lengths of silver
bells joined to each other by silver beads which awoke
in Jessica a memory of a time she seldom allowed herself to think of any more, when her parents were alive
and she was about four, and they'd all gone to her ma-
ternal grandmother's for Christmas and that house, too,
had been filled with silver bells and beads and a tall,
fragrant tree.

Discarding all the others, Jessica took this last box
into the living room and set to work. Some ornaments
she dangled precariously from the very tips of the pine's
branches, others she hid closer to the trunk where they
winked shyly among the lights.

Satisfied at last that the tree was as close to perfect as
she could make it, she arranged a few remaining blown-
glass items in a crystal bowl and set them on the coffee
table where they picked up the light from the fire and
flung it back in blazing prisms of burgundy and gold.

She polished the tarnish from silver candlesticks in

the dining room and fitted them with tall white candles she found in a drawer. She washed the dust from the beveled glass doors and left them open so that the fresh piny scent of the tree could filter through from the living room.

She swabbed cobwebs from the fine brass chandelier above the long oak table, and vacuumed the rugs back to life. And when all the furniture in both rooms glowed from her efforts she searched through the linen drawer in the bottom of the sideboard and found a big white damask cloth and a set of matching serviettes.

"It's quitting time, Jessica. Put your dust mop away and—" Morgan poked his head around the door just as she finished laying out the heavy silver she'd discovered in the silver chest. But when he saw the transformation that had taken place in the two rooms he stopped and stared, and said quietly, "Well, I'll be damned!"

Somewhat apprehensively, she said, "Is it all right?"

He shook his head wonderingly. "It's a lot better than all right." Then, raising his voice, he called out, "Clancy, come in here and take a look at what's happened!"

Jessica heard the stable man's footsteps coming down the hall and braced herself for the silent scorn he'd level at her. But when he, too, saw what she'd done his jaw went slack with amazement and, although she couldn't be certain, she thought that his eyes filmed with tears. "You brought out all Agnes's things," he said huskily. "All the little bits and pieces she made over the years that the other one shoved to one side."

Jessica glanced at Morgan, wondering if she'd inadvertently committed another unforgivable sin, but he shook his head reassuringly as Clancy slowly crossed to the tree and touched one of the crocheted snowflakes with a calloused fingertip.

"Made one of these every year, she did," he said,

half to himself. "Used to say they were for the babies God never gave her."

"She'd be glad to see them brought out again." Morgan went to stand beside him and slung an arm over his shoulder.

Clancy ignored him and switched his rheumy gaze to Jessica. "What else you gone and found, woman?"

"I...um...nothing." She indicated the table in the dining room and sent another uncertain glance winging Morgan's way. "Except for the table linens and the sterling. But if you'd rather—"

"Best get the good china out, then," Clancy declared, any trace of emotion firmly under control again. "Ain't no point doing things half-assed."

But Morgan insisted she'd done enough for one day and sent her upstairs to take a shower. When she came down again in a fresh skirt and clean blouse, the table was set, and the men were sprawled in armchairs beside the fire with the dogs at their feet, and chatting amiably. Whatever tension had sprung up between them that morning seemed long gone and they were friends again.

Morgan offered her sherry while Clancy piled another log on the fire. "Shoot, why not?" he said, dusting off his hands on the seat of his pants and accepting the glass of rye whisky Morgan had poured for him. "Reckon we're going to celebrate Christmas whether we ought to or not, so we might as well enjoy it."

The way he said "ought" struck a vaguely discordant note, as though there was something wrong with what they were doing, but Jessica wasn't about to question him on it. It was enough that he'd called off his private vendetta against her. He even unbent far enough to help clean up after dinner—"since you're so persnickety about not leaving a mess behind, woman," he said, with the closest thing to a smile yet to cross his face.

He left and took the dogs to his own quarters shortly after, going out by the front door for a change. Morgan and Jessica stood in the lee of the veranda, watching until they saw lights go on in the windows above the stables.

It had stopped snowing by then and a cold moon shone over the land, leaving the air so crystalline that it almost chimed. "Breathtaking, isn't it?" Morgan said, gazing out at the frozen grandeur spread before them.

"Yes." Jessica hunched her shoulders against the chill penetrating the thin fabric of her blouse.

He noticed and pulled her into the shelter of his arm, in an unselfconscious, brotherly sort of way that nevertheless sent a thrill of excitement charging through her. "You and your damned wardrobe," he grumbled, but there was no real annoyance in his tone any more.

"If I'd known I was going to be moon-watching in minus thirty-degree weather, I'd have brought along my full-length furs," she said, unable to control her chattering teeth.

He swung her around and led her back inside the house. "You don't own any furs," he said confidently, steering her toward the hearth.

She crouched before the fire and held out her hands to its leaping warmth. "What makes you so sure?"

"No woman who sees Rudolph on her plate instead of venison stew would stoop to wearing animal skins on her back," he said, selecting a bottle from one of the sideboard cupboards and pouring an inch of cognac into two snifters.

Jessica smiled. "Perhaps you know me better than I thought."

He handed her a cognac then lowered himself into his chair again, legs stretched out so that his feet almost touched her. "But not as much as I'm beginning to think I'd like to know you."

When she didn't reply, he nudged her with his toe. "Don't go all coy on me, Jessica. I've never enjoyed playing twenty questions."

"There's nothing much to tell." She shrugged and cradled the cognac snifter in both hands. "I have a sister, which you already know. I'm gainfully employed. I have no known allergies, don't smoke, only drink socially and then not much."

"And you're single."

"Yes," she said, and seized the chance to satisfy the most burning question she had for him. "Are you?"

He smiled lazily. "We're not talking about me and you're not going to wriggle off the hook by trying to change the subject. What line of work are you in?"

"I'm the headmistress of a private girls' school on Springhill Island in the Gulf of Georgia."

"I should have guessed!" His burst of laughter cut her to the quick. "It suits you to a T!"

Deciding she'd rather eat worms than let him see the wound he'd inflicted, she said, "Doesn't it just? Strait-laced spinster schoolmarm all the way, that's me."

He sobered, as though he'd heard something more than the words she'd tossed out so airily. "That's not exactly how I see you, Jessica."

"Why ever not?" She turned her face away from his probing stare and concentrated on the flames leaping up the chimney. "Everyone else does. I'm the plain sister, the intimidatingly sensible one. If glamor and excitement were what you'd hoped to find to brighten the season when you so kindly rescued me, I'm afraid you chose the wrong woman."

"I wasn't looking for any kind of woman," he said, leaning forward to capture her shoulders and pull her back against his knees. "But now that you're here I can't say I regret having found you."

"Because I'm such a good housekeeper," she said, despising the quaver of self-pity she heard in her voice. What a pathetic creature she was, practically begging for his approval.

She felt his breath ruffle her hair, the weight of his

chin rest on the crown of her head. "Why do you persist in selling yourself short all the time, Miss Simms?"

Why did he persist in asking questions? In talking, instead of taking advantage of the situation? They were a man and a woman alone in a house for the night, with Christmas lights spilling magic into the room and the scent of freshly cut pine in the air.

It was the perfect setting, the perfect opportunity. If Selena had been the one taking refuge in his house, he'd have kissed her by now. Probably done a lot more than kiss her, in fact. "I'm realistic, that's all. And it's not as if you were overjoyed to have me land on your doorstep."

"No," he murmured, lifting the heavy loop of her hair and caressing the back of her neck. "But that was then and this is now. As for finding you plain...."

He left the sentence dangling, which was almost worse than if he'd ended it by allowing that she couldn't help how she looked. But then, when she'd just about decided she couldn't take his ambiguous silence a moment longer, he finished, "I don't find you plain at all, Jessica. On the contrary, I find you quite irresistibly lovely."

Just for a second everything in the room seemed to hang in frozen tension, in the same way that a concert hall filled with breathless suspense as the conductor raised his baton. The pretty Christmas tree ornaments stopped twirling, the lights ceased their tiny reflective flickerings. Even the flames in the hearth grew still, their crackle silenced and their heat quite unequal to the task of outshining the sudden fire in her blood.

She held onto that moment as long as she could, then came straight out and asked him, "Are you married, Morgan?"

"No," he replied in a low voice, leaving one less hurdle between them. "Not any more."

She took a deep breath. "And do you find me intimidatingly sensible?"

"I don't intimidate that easily, Jessica."

She dared then to turn her head and look at him, because she had to read the truth in his eyes as she asked him the one question that she simply had to know the answer to. "Then why haven't you tried to make love to me?"

CHAPTER SIX

MORGAN was blown away, by the question, certainly, and the honesty that inspired it, and by the leap of arousal with which his flesh responded to it, but most of all what moved him was the utter devastation he saw in Jessica's eyes as she waited for his answer.

"Do you think the idea hasn't crossed my mind a dozen times?" he said.

She lowered her eyes then and would have turned away from him, but he forestalled her by holding her chin firmly between his thumb and finger. "No," she whispered, a delicate wash of color flooding her face. "I didn't think you'd even noticed me, except as an inconvenience that suddenly managed to make itself useful."

He looked at her helplessly, at a loss to explain how she'd grown on him over the last forty-eight hours. Could he match truth for truth and tell her that, at first, he'd seen her just as she saw herself, plain and uninteresting? Or that he'd soon recognized that she was simply shy and that, under the somewhat forbidding facade behind which she tried to hide the fact, she possessed a cool beauty, subtle as perfume skilfully applied, and just about as elusive?

He cleared his throat and wished he could as easily subdue the rest of his body. "There is every reason in the world for me not to take advantage of you," he said huskily, "and I'm probably every sort of fool to point it out, but—"

"It's all right." She closed her eyes in humiliation. "I had no right to ask. I don't know what came over me."

"You were being honest with me, Jessica, and I really would be a fool not to feel flattered, but the more important question is, were you being honest with yourself? Are you sure this is what you really want?"

She hugged her elbows, as though no amount of heat from the fire could warm her. "Not if I start to analyze it. Not if I apply judgement or rational argument. But if I obey...."

The words died on a breath of despair, as though she couldn't bring herself to admit that she was at the mercy of something that refused to abide by the laws of reason.

"What would you do," he asked, "if I said I'd be happy to oblige?"

Her eyes flew open and he saw the panic in them, the uncertainty, and underneath all that something tremulous and fragile and unbearably appealing.

He couldn't bring himself to let her flounder a moment longer. He slid from the chair to sit beside her on the floor and, cupping her cheek in his palm, added, "But that I'll act on it only if you still feel the same way twenty-four hours from now."

Her lashes fluttered down beguilingly and if he hadn't known better he'd have thought her a practiced tease. "I...don't think I could bring myself to ask a second time."

He took the brandy snifter from her hands and placed it beside his own on the hearth. "Not even if I show now, like this, how very desirable I find you?"

He tilted her chin up again and fanned the question against her mouth. She shifted ever so slightly, angling one shoulder protectively against his invasion in a gesture that stirred the warm currents of air trapped inside her blouse.

The scent of her flowed out to seduce him, country flowers and summer dawns too alluring to withstand. The kiss he'd intended to bestow as a salve to her pride ran amok with a passion he'd never anticipated and couldn't begin to contain.

Her mouth melted beneath his, so hot and fragrantly erotic that it might never have known the touch of wintry reserve he'd first seen painted there. He felt himself drowning in the essence of her, tasting the texture of her, delving deep to unearth more of her secrets.

She was all silk and sweet compliance, from the soft fringe of her lashes against her cheek to her lips, to her hair slipping free of its clasp and sliding like water through his fingers, to the skin of her throat, to the smooth slope of her breast—

Abruptly he pulled away from her, dropping her like the proverbial hot potato, too shocked by the degree of arousal she stirred in him to consider how she might view his actions.

Confused, frustrated, he flung wide both hands in an attempt to explain himself. "Forgive me. I—that's not what I—"

"Please don't," she said, visibly withdrawing into herself like a flower suddenly deprived of the sun's heat. "Please don't feel you have to apologize. I understand."

"No, you don't!" His answer exploded between them. "Hell, I don't understand myself! I intended to kiss you, that was all. I thought that would be enough and...."

He blew out a breath of exasperation and shook his head. How did a man of thirty-seven, who'd known more than a few women in his time, explain that he'd never before had a kiss sneak up and take him by surprise like that?

"It wasn't enough," he finished quietly.

"But it was very nice," she said, once again lowering her lashes fetchingly.

He almost smiled. "Are you flirting with me, Miss Simms?"

"I don't know how to flirt. I haven't had much occasion to practice."

He sighed ruefully and, picking up the brandy snifters again, offered her hers. "I suspect you'd be a very quick study."

"I'm not sure that I'd want to be," she said seriously. "I think, if ever I were to find myself involved with a man, that I'd rather play it straight. Flirting..." she lifted a disparaging shoulder "...it can lead to trouble, don't you think?"

He leaned his spine against the chair and crossed his ankles. "What sort of trouble?"

"Things can get out of hand. And then, when it's too late, people can find they've done irreparable damage."

Yes, he thought, just as Gabriel Parrish had.

Ill wind that it was, the name blasted across Morgan's mind, scattering everything else before it. Where the hell did he get off even contemplating an involvement with this woman when a madman was on the loose and probably out gunning for him?

She was so painfully honest, and all he had to offer her were lies. But what else could he do? Say "I'd make love to you in a New York minute, sweetheart, but you should be aware we could both be murdered in the bed"?

No. If he cared at all about her—and he was beginning to think he did, more than he wanted or had expected to—he'd leave her in ignorance and, more to the point, ensure her protection.

Draining his glass, he rose swiftly to his feet, gripped by a sudden need to check around outside, to make sure they were all safe, at least for one more night. "I could use some fresh air before I turn in and you must be worn out, the way you've slaved today." Quickly, before the pain so evident in her eyes had him sweeping her into his arms again, he turned away from her. "Get a good night's rest and I'll see you in the morning."

* * *

He took all the warmth of the room with him when he left.

Left? Practically ran out, as if he couldn't wait to get away from her, was a more apt description!

Shame and embarrassment flooded through Jessica, leaving her trembling and on the verge of tears. How *could* she have said what she did?

She looked down at the cognac in her glass and wished she could blame it for the words that had escaped her, but the fact of the matter was she'd hardly touched the liquor and had nothing and no one to blame but herself.

Was this what she'd come to? she wondered, standing up only to find that her legs threatened to give out under her. Was she so desperate to feel a man's arms around her again that she was willing to beg?

And yet the way he'd kissed her...the hunger hadn't been all hers. Nor was she so ignorant that she couldn't recognize the desire he hadn't been able to disguise. She'd felt him, hard and powerful against her. Had heard, over the labored thud of her heart, the rasp of his breath as he'd struggled to control himself.

If she had dared trust her instinct, she'd have guessed that he'd told her the truth when he'd said that he wanted her. But intuition, at least where men were concerned, had let her down too badly for her to have much faith in it a second time, especially on so brief an acquaintance.

This hunger, this raw animal magnetism, was a new experience for her and she was terribly afraid it had clouded her judgement. The only other time she'd come close to feeling anything like it had been with Stuart McKinney. She'd believed herself in love with him and thought that justified the physical side of things, only to learn that love didn't necessarily have anything to do with sex.

She'd decided then that she'd never again barter her

body to win affection, and she'd never had reason to think otherwise, until now. But Morgan Kincaid...oh, he made her wish she were different, better, braver. He awoke the secret woman inside her and made her yearn and ache and want.

"Idiot," she whispered, and stooped to unplug the tree lights, then took the brandy snifters into the kitchen before she went upstairs. Leaving the bedroom in darkness, she crossed to the window and looked out at the snow-covered landscape glimmering beneath the moon.

She saw the shadow of him emerge from the dark bulk of the stables, watched as he stood at the foot of the veranda steps and surveyed his quiet kingdom. And knew again a wave of sadness that she could be a part of his life for such a short space of time.

He had already left the house when she ventured downstairs the next morning, and for that she was supremely grateful. It was going to be hard enough facing him, without having to do it over the breakfast table. She was not at her best before her first cup of coffee of the day.

She made short work of cleaning up the kitchen and was on her hands and knees in the living room, adding fresh water to the Christmas tree container, when the back door suddenly thumped open long before the men usually took their mid-morning coffee break.

Her heart almost cartwheeled to a halt but it was Clancy, not Morgan, who appeared next to her with a pile of slender evergreen branches in his arms. "Figured since you done such a fancy job on the tree that you'd want to dolly up the rest of the place," he said offhandedly, dumping his load on the freshly vacuumed rug. "Got some cedar here that I cut first thing. Agnes used to put it on the mantelpiece—left it sort of hanging over the edge—and it always looked real nice."

Jessica sat back on her heels and eyed him cautiously, bowled over by the about-face that had produced such a gesture of goodwill. "Thank you. That's a wonderful idea."

"There's holly growing out back as well. In the corner where the kitchen sticks out, where it's sheltered from the worst of the weather. Not that it's got any right growing at this altitude, but the darn thing's as stubborn as the old gal that planted it."

"Agnes?" It seemed a reasonable guess since he was so full of memories of her, but Jessica soon learned her mistake.

"Use your head, woman," Clancy snorted. "Trees don't grow like weeds, 'specially not up here, and my Agnes was only sixty-six when she passed on. I'm talking about Morgan's great-granny. A real green thumb, she had. Got things to sprout that folks around these parts never did see before. Always had holly in the house at Christmas. Thought you might like some, too."

"I would, but it can wait. You've already got enough to do."

"That I have." He glared at Jessica, as though his bringing her one peace offering had stretched his capacity for seasonal goodwill to its limit.

"Perhaps I could cut some myself later on," she offered.

"Not dressed like that, you can't." He sniffed. "Woman, you've been here nearly three days and you still ain't got the first idea what that weather out there can do to a person who don't come equipped to deal with it."

She sighed. She was getting more than a little tired of being chastised for her inadequate wardrobe. What she wore seemed the preferred topic of conversation, losing out only to the current state of the weather. "Well, Clancy, I'm learning fast. However, since there's nothing I can do to remedy the situation, I guess we'll all just have to live—"

"Ain't no call for you to get on your high and mighty

horse,'' he said, cocking his head to one side and squinting at her. ''All I was goin' to suggest was that from where I stand you look to be about the same size as my Agnes and if you ain't too proud to take hand-me-downs maybe I can fix you up with something so you ain't quite so housebound.''

''That would be very nice,'' she said, deeming it unwise to take exception to the way he chose to deliver his point.

He left then, slamming the back door in his signature fashion, only to return half an hour later with a large cardboard box which he plunked in the middle of the sofa. ''There. See what you can do with what's in here. The boots might be big but that ain't nothing an extra pair of socks can't fix.'' He nodded and turned to go, then asked, ''By the way, what you cooking up for the midday meal?''

''Grilled cheese sandwiches and tomato soup.''

''And some of them mince pie things like we had yesterday?''

''If you like. I'll have to bake up a fresh batch, though.''

She smiled at him and received a conspiratorial smirk in response. ''Better get on with it, then, woman. I'm building up a fearsome appetite running errands for you.''

Although she felt better at the improved turn her relationship with Clancy had taken, Jessica still dreaded seeing Morgan again and grew increasingly tense as the lunch hour approached. It was all she could do not to turn tail and run when she heard the clump of boots at the back door. But after all her agonizing he made it easy for her.

''Hi,'' he said, planting himself at the table and rubbing his hands together briskly. ''What's cooking? I'm starving.''

His smile was friendly without being intimate, his

glance impersonal without being cold, his tone weighted with no hidden nuances. He was so thoroughly and neutrally pleasant that it occurred to Jessica to wonder if she hadn't dreamed the previous night's conversation.

"Heard on the radio this morning that there was another avalanche on the main highway," he commented as the meal progressed. "Just west of Wintercreek this time. They don't expect to have the road open again for at least forty-eight hours."

Clancy, who until then had attacked his meal with the same silent dedication he'd displayed the day before, froze with his sandwich midway to his mouth. "That ought to put a dent in certain folks' traveling plans."

"I'd say so." Morgan smiled his thanks as Jessica removed his empty soup bowl. "At least until after Christmas Day."

"Speaking of which," she said, producing the promised mince tarts, "unless you've got it hidden somewhere, I don't see any sign of the traditional turkey for tomorrow's dinner."

Morgan intercepted Clancy as he made a grab for the tarts. "We didn't bother with one last year. It didn't seem worth it for just the two of us."

"So what did you have in mind instead?"

"We laid in a good supply of wild duck in the Fall. They're in the freezer but if they don't strike your fancy whatever you decide will be fine." He shrugged apologetically. "Christmas Day's just another working day on a horse ranch, Jessica. I'm afraid you'll be spending a good portion of it alone, doing exactly the same thing you've done so well since you got here."

"Pinch-hitting as chief cook and bottle washer, you mean?" She spoke idly, too deeply engrossed in admiring the lithe male beauty of him to consider how her words might be interpreted.

Unexpectedly, he looked up and caught her staring.

"Among other things," he said gently, his gaze holding hers.

Did she imagine that his expression altered imperceptibly, that the color of his eyes suddenly reminded her less of the clear cold of the winter sky than the hazy blue of high summer?

"Well," she said, hoping the confusion churning her blood didn't show on her face, "wild duck sounds fine to me. I'll do my best to make them special."

His gaze intensified. "As you do with everything, Jessica."

"Anybody want to tell me what the Sam hell all the double talk's about?" Clancy inquired, not missing a thing. "Or am I better off not knowin'?"

"You're better off not knowing," Morgan said evenly. "What say we get back to work?"

"Might as well. Sooner we get at it, sooner we're done." Clancy scraped back his chair and snapped the leather suspenders holding up his jeans. "A man sits too long by a warm fire lettin' a woman feed him and next thing you know he ain't good for nothin' the rest of the day."

"Then by all means let's get moving." Standing up, Morgan slewed his gaze briefly back to Jessica and with a masterful stroke of ambiguity that sent a tide of heat sweeping over her added slyly, "You look a little weary, Miss Simms. Why don't you take time out for a nap this afternoon? It would be a pity for either of us to be too tired to enjoy Christmas Eve."

Clancy snorted with disgust, snaked out a hand and crammed the last mince pie into his mouth whole. "Never mind any afternoon nap, woman," he said, heading for the door. "Make more tarts."

By great good fortune, Agnes had been a size eight, too. Her faded blue jeans, softened by many launderings to the texture of doeskin, fit perfectly. Sorting through the

other items, Jessica selected a hand-knit sweater that
came down past her hips, a cream down jacket with a
fur-trimmed hood, two pairs of heavy wool socks to
wear under the fleece-lined boots, and a pair of thick
leather gloves. But she shook her head at the long red
thermal underwear and tucked it back inside the box.
She didn't plan to spend any longer outside than it took
to gather a few pieces of holly.

The problem was, whatever tool Clancy had used to
cut the cedar was nowhere to be found and the holly
branches were sturdy as well as prickly. The kitchen
scissors were no match for the job, nor was the steak
knife she seconded. Frustrated and out of breath, she
surveyed the bright-berried limb dangling miserably but
stubbornly from the tree. Obviously, without the proper
tools, she wasn't going to have much success.

"Stay inside the house", Morgan had said. But the
stables stood a mere hundred yards or so away. Hardly
a life-threatening distance, now that she had the right
kind of clothing to protect her, surely?

But the cold wind from which she'd been protected
by the bulk of the house caught her as she turned the
corner and just about froze the breath in her lungs. Hug-
ging the jacket hood closely around her face and wishing
she hadn't been so quick to discard Agnes's winter underwear, she struggled across the open ground to the
stable and slid back the heavy door just enough to let
herself through the opening.

Her arrival went unnoticed at first and for a moment
she leaned against the door and simply inhaled the gentle
warmth of the place. A window high on the end wall let
in what was left of the daylight and two electric lamps
suspended from a center beam spilled mellow pools of
gold over the scene.

Shadowed stalls lined each side wall, five to the left
and five to the right, with a concrete-floored aisle separating them. Steps immediately to the right of the door

by which she'd come in led up to a half-loft piled high
with bales of bright straw and pale-tinted hay.

To her left, another half-open door showed a small
room, the walls of which were hung with the trappings
one might expect to find around horses. Saddles and bri-
dles, blankets and liniments, oils and brushes.

The entire place was filled with the scents of hay and
clean straw and the faintly astringent smell of animals.
The air was full of soft sound: hooves rustling on straw,
contented munching, water gurgling down twin drinking
channels, and somewhere out of sight the deep baritone
murmur of men at work together.

Something about the place—the hushed tranquillity
perhaps, or the far window, stained now with the deep
blue of the midwinter afternoon and shot with rose from
the dying sun—reminded her of a church. To call out
and shatter the peace was unthinkable.

Hesitantly, she moved forward, toward the sound of
voices, aware all the time of the horses. Some looked
up from their feeding troughs, mildly curious, then dismissed her for the ignorant intruder she undoubtedly
was. Others whickered softly and watched her with
large, beautiful eyes as she made her way down the center aisle.

She had almost reached the last stall when a low growl
issued from an old blanket atop a pile of straw and Ben
the retriever rose up to confront her.

"Stop that," she scolded softly, coming to a halt a
respectful distance away—not that she was afraid of him
exactly, but nor was she fool enough to challenge him
on his own turf. "I'm the one who fed you venison stew
for the last two days, you ungrateful wretch."

He growled again, loudly enough this time for the
men to hear him. There was a moment of complete silence that positively hummed with unspoken threat and
then, suddenly, they were there, practically on top of her,
Clancy picking up a wicked-looking pitchfork hanging

on the end wall and brandishing it fiercely, and Morgan swinging a hammer.

When they saw her, they stopped their headlong rush and froze in their tracks. "Oh," Morgan said, looking somewhat embarrassed, "it's you."

"It's a bit too early for Santa Claus," she said lightly, "so who else could it be but me?"

The men exchanged furtive glances. "Well..." Morgan began.

"Horse thieves," Clancy said, his pitchfork still held at the ready.

"It pays to be careful," Morgan said.

"I'm sure." Jessica nodded her understanding, although in truth she thought their reaction rather extreme, particularly since they both continued to regard her as if she'd sprouted horns.

Morgan took off his hat and drew the back of his hand across his brow. "Is everything all right at the house, Jessica?"

"Of course. Why wouldn't it be?"

"Then what you doin' wanderin' around in here, woman?" Clancy demanded.

"Looking for something to cut the holly with," she said. "And I'm sorry if I'm trespassing, but I thought you might be able to give me something that would do the job."

"Oh," Morgan said again. "Sure. Of course. And you're not trespassing. Not at all. Put the pitchfork away, Clancy, before someone gets hurt."

"You might call off Ben, too," Jessica said.

Signaling the dog to heel, Morgan said, "A better idea would be for the two of you to become friends, then he could keep you company at the house while we're out here."

"I haven't exactly had time to get lonely, Morgan, but if you think a little company would be good for me Shadow seems much more inclined to be friendly and is perfectly happy to spend the day with me. She's asleep in the rocking chair even as we speak.''

Again, that silent exchange took place between the men. "Yeah," Clancy muttered, "but Ben's more...."

"Territorial," Morgan supplied.

Jessica regarded them quizzically. "In the event that horse thieves should invade the kitchen in the middle of the day, of course."

"You're right, we're making a fuss about nothing. I guess having you show up so quietly surprised us, that's all." Morgan shrugged and relaxed his grip on the hammer. "I'm about done for today anyway, so why don't I walk back to the house with you?"

"What about cutting the holly?"

"I'll do it. You shouldn't be outside dressed like—" He stopped and seemed to notice what she was wearing for the first time. "Where did you get the clothes, for Pete's sake?"

"From me. They're some of Agnes's things that I'd kept," Clancy said. "Reckon I'll poultice the mare's ankle before I quit for the day, Morgan, 'less you got something else you want me to do?"

Morgan shook his head. "I think we've covered everything."

"What's wrong with the mare?" Jessica asked in a low voice, glancing back over her shoulder as Clancy disappeared into the end stall again.

"Sprained ankle." Morgan took her by the elbow and pointed her back the way she'd come. "Nothing too serious."

"I thought leg injuries to horses were always serious."

"Not necessarily. Come on, let's get you back to the house. This isn't exactly your sort of place, I'm sure."

"Perhaps not, but I can see why Clancy prefers to spend his time here. There's something very comforting about your stable. And the animals...." She turned to him and smiled. "He was right, you know—Clancy, I mean. I barely know the back end of a horse from the front, but even I can see they're beautiful. What do you do with them?"

A grin twitched the corners of his mouth. "Well, I don't eat them if that's what's worrying you. You won't find horse-meat steaks in the freezer."

She slapped at his arm with her gloved hand. "The thought never even occurred to me! What I meant was, are they racehorses, or do you keep them just for the pleasure of watching them run about the property?"

"Mostly the latter, I guess." He stopped and stroked the long, soft nose of a horse hanging its head over the half-door of its stall. "They're quarter horses and I do a bit of breeding. And a lot of riding when I can spare the time. But this is a small operation compared to what it was in my grandfather's day, and that's how I like it. With the part-time help he gets from Ted, Clancy's able to manage the place single-handed if I'm not around, although we do employ some of the local kids during the summer."

The horse nudged at his chest and sort of snuffled, a move that had Jessica springing back in alarm. "Good grief, is he going to bite?"

It seemed a reasonable enough question to her, but Morgan just about split his sides laughing. "No, sweetheart, he's looking for something to eat. Do you want to feed him?"

"Not if he's that hungry," she retorted, too fired up with pleasure at the endearment to resent his teasing. "I might lose my hand."

Looping one arm around her shoulder, Morgan reached into his pocket with his other hand and withdrew a carrot. "No chance of that," he assured her. "Not if you do it right. Here, take off your glove and lay this flat on the palm of your hand."

"Can't I keep my glove on?"

"No. You lose half the pleasure."

Taking courage from that casually uttered "sweetheart" and the arm around her shoulder, she removed her glove.

"Now offer him the carrot. Go on," Morgan urged, when she hesitated. The horse had lost all interest in his owner and was eyeing her with alarming enthusiasm.

"Morgan," she said, "that animal and I haven't been properly introduced and considering how Ben responds to me I'm not sure I'm willing to trust anything quite this big even if he is the most handsome shade of brown I've ever seen."

"He's a chestnut," Morgan corrected her. "His name's Jasper, he's nearly sixteen years old and he's never hurt a fly in all that time. And you're offending him by suggesting he would."

Conscious of the big brown eyes watching her so patiently, and even more vividly aware of the brilliant blue gaze of the man at her side, Jessica raised her arm.

The great head dipped in a bow to her outstretched palm. She felt a touch, gentle as a kiss, the feathery brush of whiskers, and the carrot was gone.

"Well? How was it?"

Her smile completely got away from her, spreading past its normal reserved boundaries with a keen pleasure she rarely experienced. "Piece of cake," she boasted, and suddenly she was leaning against him and they were both laughing.

"I'll make a horsewoman out of you yet," he promised, sliding the stable door shut behind them and hurrying her across the snow-packed path to the house.

He cut the holly while she made tea, then took his cup into his office. "I've got a couple of hours' work to take care of in here before we start celebrating Christmas. Can you keep yourself occupied while you're waiting?"

"Easily," she said, and idled the rest of the afternoon

away doing little, inconsequential things. She studded mandarin oranges with whole cloves, piled them in a pewter bowl with pine cones, and set them on the hearth where the warmth from the fire would draw out the scent. She ironed the ribbons she'd found among the decorations and wove them in graceful swirls through the sprigs of holly and sprays of cedar gracing the dining table and fringing the mantelpiece.

She felt it was the sort of thing Agnes would have wanted her to do: to bring the added dimension of a woman's touch to the house and turn it again into a home. And the house responded, seeming to expand at the seams and let loose ghosts from a happier time.

As darkness closed in outside, she basted the potatoes roasting around the leg of pork in the oven, set plates to warm, opened preserved peaches and, in preparation for the ice cream dessert she had planned, left them to marinate drunkenly in a sauce made of brown sugar, raisins and dark rum.

When she came downstairs later, all bathed and perfumed and wearing one of only two dresses she'd stuffed in her suitcase, she found Clancy pumping away on the old organ and filling the room with the wheezing strains of "Silent Night".

In the corner, the lights on the tree winked softly. Beyond the beveled glass doors, candles flickered in the dining room. On the coffee table before the fire sat a fine old silver punch bowl with three matching cups. And best of all there was Morgan, gorgeous in black cords and a white shirt.

She paused a moment on the threshold, wondering a little at the sensation suddenly engulfing her. Airy, translucent and thoroughly unfamiliar, it flooded through her and she realized, with a sense of shock, what it was she was experiencing.

Not satisfaction for a job well done. Not contented gratitude for a pleasant, secure life. But happiness that surged and flowed through her veins with all the verve and delight of champagne sparkling on the tongue.

There were no smartly wrapped packages under the tree, no uniformed staff hired for the evening. No stream of fashionably clad guests streaming through the front door as they had in her aunt and uncle's house, air-kissing each other's cheeks at the same time that they took covert stock of who was wearing what and designed by whom.

Just Christmas the way it was meant to be: warm, unpretentious, *real*.

CHAPTER SEVEN

MORGAN ladled out hot rum punch but before he could propose a toast Clancy upstaged him. Shuffling around on the organ stool, he clutched the delicate punch cup in his big hands.

"Never thought I'd feel like this again," he began, scanning the room at large. "Never thought it would feel like a home again." He focused his attention on Jessica. "For sure never thought a bit of a woman'd just walk in the door and make the place over in three days."

His expression was almost bewildered and it struck Morgan that his stable hand had aged over the last few months and now looked all of his sixty-eight years.

"'Specially not a woman like you, Jessica Simms," Clancy continued. "Wouldn't have thought you had it in you to pull off something like this." He raised his cup. "Best of the season to you. My Agnes would have approved of you."

"I know I would have liked her, too." Emotion clogged Jessica's voice, undershot her smile, and left her gray eyes sparkling with the hint of tears.

Morgan would have preferred not to notice any of those revealing little details but the more time he spent in her company, the more acute his powers of observation became. And the lovelier she grew.

He continued to observe her over dinner, noticing the thoroughbred elegance of her, her warmth, her patience with Clancy. She'd grown younger somehow, as if she'd shed the weight of countless years of disappointment and unhappiness. Or, more accurately, as if, since knowing him, she'd discovered joy.

How would it have been between them, he wondered, if he'd met her before? Before a failed marriage had taught him there were some things you couldn't ask a woman to do, such as live with a man who made enemies of creeps like Gabriel Parrish?

He tried to picture her in that world now, and failed. It had proved to be too much for Daphne and, in the end, it would be too much for Jessica, too. She wasn't hard-edged enough.

No. If ever there'd been a time for them, it was ten years ago, before they had each laid out their lives along different paths.

"You've made a conquest," he told her later, slouching comfortably beside her on the couch. Dinner was over and Clancy had retired to his own quarters a short while before, again leaving the two of them alone to finish the last of the wine they'd drunk with the meal. "I don't recall Clancy ever waxing quite so lyrical before."

"My cooking mellows him." Jessica smiled, a shade wistfully, he thought. As if the only possible route she'd find to a man's heart lay through his stomach.

If he could limit his susceptibility to her to such an innocuous portion of his anatomy, Morgan decided, leaning forward and cradling his wine glass in both hands, he'd feel a lot more relaxed about the situation in which he now found himself.

"So I've noticed," he said. "Come to that, I've noticed a lot of things in the last couple of days that escaped me when we first met."

"Such as?" She crossed one knee over the other and swung a graceful ankle. The fabric of her full-skirted dress, something thick and silky printed with dark green ferns on a cream background, flowed onto his section of the couch, begging to be touched.

Fixing his attention on the cedar garland festooned

along the mantel, he said, "Initially, I had you pegged as being a bit hare-brained, a bit irresponsible."

"And now you know I'm just a staid old schoolmarm you think differently?"

"It's not your job that changed my mind."

She shifted to a more comfortable position, sliding lower against the cushions and sending a faint whiff of perfumed body talc drifting his way. "What, then?"

The fact that the scent of you drives me mad, he could have told her. That when you stretch out your foot like that, letting your heel slip free of its shoe, I have an insane urge to kneel down and kiss that high, aristocratic instep. That you have beautiful legs, slender, shapely and endless, and I'd like to explore them at erotic leisure. That there's a sliver of French lace showing beneath the hem of your dress and it brings to mind the nightgown you were wearing the other night, and has me wondering what you're wearing next to your skin now—all of which speculation has left me seriously aroused.

"Search me!" he said.

And wouldn't *that* be embarrassing!

Leaping to his feet, he threw another log on the fire with rather more energy than the task demanded. "Your unselfishness, perhaps. You'd never have ended up stranded in a blizzard if you hadn't set out in the middle of one of the worst winters on record to be with your sister. And if we hadn't roped you into housekeeping for a couple of bachelors whose idea of celebrating Christmas runs to propping up a tree in a corner and forgetting to water it, Clancy and I would probably be staring at the bottom of an empty brandy bottle about now, bemoaning our sad and lonely lot in life."

"I can relate to that."

He flung a skeptical glance at her over his shoulder. "What, getting hammered on brandy?"

The way she leaned against the arm of the couch and tilted one shoulder in an unwittingly sensuous shrug of denial that brought her arm into brief and intimate contact with her breast sent a tongue of fire curling through his gut.

"No," she said. "Being sad and lonely. It's just something that comes of being the sort of person I am, I guess."

If she'd evidenced even a shred of self-pity with that remark, he could have dismissed her claim, ignored it, laughed at it. Responded in any number of ways, in fact, but the way he did, which was to ignore his better judgement and submit instead to the urge that had gnawed at him incessantly for the last twenty-four hours or more.

Taking her hands, he drew her to her feet and held her close. "Not tonight it isn't," he murmured into her hair.

She came to him as naturally as if she'd found shelter in his arms a thousand times before. Her head rested below his chin, the scent of her which, across the width of the couch, had spelled faint temptation intensified to vibrant invitation. And the rest of her, every fine-boned, delicately sculpted inch of limb and torso, imprinted itself against him.

It was more than he'd anticipated or planned, yet it left him craving for more. The belief which had served him so long and so well that love was, at best, a transient visitor and not worth the upheaval it created threatened to topple into a great yawning abyss of need.

Love? How the hell had that word slipped through his defenses? He wasn't a good candidate for love and, even if he were, Jessica deserved better. Her life was bound by purer standards than he could afford, her definitions of right and wrong too clearly spelled out in black and white.

How could she understand the many shadings of gray that governed him? How accept the necessity of his sometimes rubbing shoulders with the underworld of crime in order to bring a felon to justice?

She would not. And yet he found himself increasingly enthralled by her. Found himself waiting to hear her laugh; to see amusement shimmer over her face and fill her eyes with light; to enjoy her intelligence and her sometimes acerbic wit. These aroused in him a yearning that would not find ease in sex.

He wanted more. He wanted to take her out in public, show her off to his friends and associates, and to strangers, too, come to that. He wanted to wine and dine her, and proclaim to the world that she belonged to him. The knowledge hit him like a brick wall.

Even as his mind scrambled to absorb the realization, his body again advertised itself with blatant effrontery. Hers swayed in response. She sighed dreamily, lifted her face to his, and any scruples he might have brought to bear on the situation fled.

Sliding his hands down to cup her hips, he brought her more familiarly against him and lowered his mouth to hers. She tasted of sun-ripened grapes fermented to ambrosia, of innocence and sweetness and dark feminine mystery.

She kissed like no woman had ever kissed him before, in a way that had the alarm bells clanging at the back of his mind fighting a losing battle with the pulsing throb of his beleaguered body.

Her lips softened and parted on a whisper. Her tongue, shy as a butterfly, flirted with his, luring him to claim deeper possession of her mouth, and only when it was much too late for him to retreat, enslaving him for as long as it pleased her.

She slipped her arms around his neck and captured his hair in her fingers. Worse, she wove lethal, invisible strands around his heart.

Her flesh was warm and firm beneath his touch, but too well protected by her clothing. Sinking with her to the couch again, he inched up the skirt of her dress and traced the sweet curve of her knee, discovered the tender

inner sweep of her silk-stockinged thigh and then, unexpectedly, a strip of naked skin, enticingly soft, unbearably arousing.

Instinctively she clamped her thighs together, trapping
his hand next to the damp, delicious warmth of her, and
uttered a little moan of despair—an admission that she
was his for the taking.

He'd had his share of women and liked to think there
wasn't much that was new or different that he'd yet to
learn, but the profoundly erotic effect of that two inches
of neutral territory separating him from her most intimate self rocked him to the foundations.

Briefly, lamentably, the atavistic urge to take her then
and there, to imprint her with the mark of his possession,
blew all other considerations aside. Never mind the wide
bed upstairs, never mind chivalry or dignity, and to hell
with politically correct. The here and now was what mattered. Urgency raced through his blood, consigning finesse to some other day, some other woman.

But she was not some other woman. She was different, finer. That she was willing to give herself to him
was immaterial. Did that give him the right to take her,
knowing as he did that, when tomorrow came, he'd have
nothing of worth to offer her?

Had he not known the answer, he could have ignored
the question. But there was a limit, even to his wilful
oversight. Dearly though the effort cost him, he dragged
his mouth from hers, grasped her shoulders, and held her
at a safe distance.

"This is madness," he muttered, the breath rasping
unevenly from his lungs.

Eyes still closed, she leaned toward him. "No," she
breathed.

"Yes!" He gave her a shake, just sharp enough to
snap her back to reality. "Look, Jessica, despite what
you said last night—"

He felt her withdrawal even before she moved, and

experienced a perverse disappointment as the magic of the moment disintegrated into a thousand shattered pieces.

"Please let's not spoil Christmas Eve by bringing that up," she begged, backing away from him.

"I think we must," he said, figuring that as long as they were talking he couldn't get into too much trouble. "The fact is, it's altogether too easy to...act on—"

But talking wasn't so safe, after all. Afraid that, unless he phrased things carefully, he'd end up making matters worse than they already were, he stumbled to find the right words—an uncommon occurrence for him. If he could marshal convincing arguments for a jury, why not for her?

But how did a man say, Look, we're here alone, the mood is right, and we've been attracted to each other practically from the word go. I'd very much like to make love to you but you're not my usual type and I'm afraid I can't live up to what you'd expect of me afterwards?

"Yes, Morgan? Go on."

Conscious of her unwavering scrutiny, he floundered on. "Well, it would be easy to get carried away by what we're feeling right now...et cetera."

"Et cetera," she echoed, her breast rising and falling on another sigh. "Of course, et cetera. I understand exactly what you mean."

She turned away, the droop of her head and her profile, illuminated by the fire's glow, a statement in themselves that she accepted his rejection of her. He should have rejoiced at being so easily let off the hook. Instead, the knot of desire tightened within him, leaving him aching for her.

"Do you?" he replied gloomily. "I wish I did."

The ghost of a smile touched her mouth. "It's the loneliness factor," she said. "It can bring the most unsuitable couples together, especially at this time of year, and fool them so that they can't always tell the difference between it and real attraction.''

"True." He seized on the excuse as a drowning man might cling to a life raft. "And being cooped up together like this doesn't help."

"I know."

He sneaked a glance at the clock on the mantel, hoping it was late enough that, under the pretext of needing to get some sleep, he could race upstairs and take a long, cold shower. But he saw with dismay that it was only eight-thirty. Too early for bed and much too late to believe they could while away the next couple of hours in idle chit-chat.

Stymied, he paced to the window and stared out. The wind which had wreaked such freezing havoc for the last forty-eight hours had blown itself out finally and taken the clouds with it.

"We could go for a walk," he suggested, on a burst of inspiration. "A breath of fresh air might do us good." *Not to mention achieve the same results as a cold shower!*

She looked doubtfully at the silky stuff of her dress, her narrow, elegant pumps. "I'll freeze to death."

"Not if you borrow Agnes's long johns," he said. "They'll keep the frost away."

And him! He well remembered seeing Agnes's red, one-piece winter underwear hanging on the drying rack in the mud room. It was enough to deflate any man's overactive libido.

The night was clear and beautiful. Stars peppered the sky, brighter, larger and more numerous than any she'd ever seen on the coast. A sliver of rising moon showed beyond the lip of the cliff behind the house. Underfoot, the snow gleamed, deceptively smooth and soft to look at, but hard as pavement to touch.

"This way," Morgan said, his breath ballooning out

in front of him. "There's a trail through the trees that leads to a lake where we swim in the summer."

Jessica shivered despite the warmth of Agnes's clothing and huddled deeper into the down-filled jacket. "I find it hard to believe it could ever get hot enough for swimming up here."

He laughed. "Temperatures can run into the low thirties in July—and I'm talking centigrade. Believe me, there've been times when the lake's felt more like a bath than a swimming hole."

"We", he kept saying, as if the place was so full of memories of his ex-wife that, divorced or not, she was still a part of his life.

The Jessica Simms who'd set out from the coast a mere four days ago would have refused to gratify the irrational jealousy inspired by such a revealing little slip. But that woman had gone astray in an avalanche shed in the middle of nowhere, and the one who'd taken her place possessed none of her reticence. *She* came right out and asked, "Your wife loved it here as well, then?"

He let out a grunt of sound, too bitter to be called laughter though that was undoubtedly what he'd intended. "Hell, no, she hated it! She hated everything about life with me."

"Then why on earth did the two of you marry?"

"Why does anyone get married?"

"Well," the new, impertinent Jessica replied, "sometimes because there's a baby on the way and, from what I've seen, you—"

"Tend to behave as if I've got no more control over my hormones than I have over the weather?" His laughter this time was laced with self-mockery.

"No!" She drew in an appalled breath. "I was going to say, you strike me as the kind of man who'd honor his obligations."

The amusement slipped away, replaced by a gravity that bordered on the austere. "There was no baby, either before or after the wedding vows," he said flatly, "but there was sex and I suppose we both mistook that for love."

"That's a terribly cynical thing to say, Morgan."

He turned a long, level stare on her as they made their way over the frozen snow toward the belt of trees to the west. "I'm a cynical man, Jessica, at least where romantic love is concerned. It's not a good investment, especially not for someone like me."

In other words, Don't make the mistake of thinking that my kissing you was the prelude to a serious commitment. She heard the warning behind his words and refused to heed it. "Just because your marriage went sour is no reason to give up on love."

"It's not just my marriage that convinced me," he said, helping her over a particularly icy patch of ground. "The private lives of too many of my...associates are littered with the same sort of casualties, some of them involving children. At least Daphne and I didn't add that crime to our list of spectacular failures."

Jessica knew that the ranch was his home, a place he loved, and she couldn't picture him anywhere else. He seemed so in tune with the solitude, so content with the unchanging pattern of days spent caring for his horses. Yet just for a second she had the feeling that there was another part of his life that he didn't want to reveal to her.

"Is working the ranch a full-time career for you, Morgan?" she asked.

"Isn't it enough?"

"Possibly. But you mentioned associates just now and I—"

"Well, I'm not the only rancher in the area, so of course I have associates. Don't we all?"

Although he spoke lightly, she sensed a reluctance to pursue the topic further that was borne out when he abruptly changed the subject. "See ahead, where the trees thin out?"

He lifted his arm and pointed. In a clearing lay the lake, a keyhole-shaped body of water whose frozen surface glimmered in the ghostly light. Around its perimeter the dark sentinels of conifers speared the sky.

"It looks magical," Jessica breathed, captivated. "A place of enchantment untouched by the ills of the mortal world."

"It's muddy on the bottom, a haven for mosquitoes in the spring, and the fishing's lousy, but...." Morgan stamped a path through the snow and grinned. "Yeah, I guess you could call it magical. We spent a lot of happy hours here when we were growing up. Learned to swim and water-ski and skate."

"Who's 'we'?" There, it was out at last, the question she'd been itching to ask.

"My sister and I."

She waited for him to elaborate, to fill in the huge blanks of his past for her. Instead, he said, "You skate, Jessica?"

"Not since I was about four. I don't imagine that counts for much."

He took her hand and drew her down to the lake's edge. "Let's find out."

"What—? Morgan, no!" She hung back, realizing what he had in mind. "I can't."

"Sure you can. It's like riding a bike; you never forget how." Slithering the last few feet down the sloping bank, he pulled her after him.

"We don't even have skates," she protested, dragging her feet. "And what if the ice can't hold our weight?"

"You're chicken." Letting go of her, he stuck out his elbows, flapped his bent arms up and down, and pushed off onto the ice, squawking like a demented rooster the whole time.

"I'm sensible," she called out, laughing. "One of us has to be."

"I'm sneaky," he replied, returning to his starting point with surprising speed. "Come on, Miss Simms. It's lesson time."

Before she could back out of range, he grabbed both her hands and, backing out onto the ice again, towed her after him, willy-nilly.

"Care to dance?" he asked, slipping his right arm around her waist.

Choking with laughter, she said, "I hardly think—!"

He cut her off by breaking into a terribly off-key rendition of "The Skaters' Waltz" and spinning her wildly around the ice.

It was absurd, an adolescent lark that they were both too old to indulge in, and they should both have fallen on their faces. But he kept them firmly upright and the moon shone down on them and another kind of magic took hold.

Slowly his singing and her laughter died and the only sound to split the night was the rustle of their feet on the ice. Slowly, it, too, faded into silence.

His hands came up and closed around her upper arms, imprisoning her far too close to him for safety. Against her will she allowed her gaze to lock with his.

For one long, trembling moment that threatened to outlast eternity, they stared into each other's eyes. The messages, floodlit by the moon's pale radiance, were plain enough to understand.

She saw torment and indecision in those deep blue, soul-searching eyes of his, and a raw masculine hunger that stole her breath away. And she knew that he read longing in hers, and the wanting that refused to go ignored.

The blood thundered in her ears, echoing the frenzied beat of her heart. Her breasts, flattened against his chest, surged alive, the ache that brought her nipples into stark relief spiraling down to clench her flesh in pleasure. And nothing, not even the barrier of heavy winter clothing, could disguise his response to her as he pressed against her, hard, forceful, male.

But mostly it was their breathing that gave them away, erupting in harsh, jagged gasps to mate plainly and deliriously in the cold night air. Writhing, coiling, becoming one.

As she longed to do with him.

As she was sure he longed to do with her. She felt the fight go out of him in the way his shoulders sagged beneath her touch, read the terms of his surrender in the way his lashes drooped and his gaze fastened on her mouth.

The silence spoke for itself, cutting through all the subterfuge to reveal the truth they'd both tried to ignore. It screamed between them, deafening in its tacit admission.

He slackened his grip enough to hold her at arm's length. "You see?" he whispered hoarsely. "This is what I was trying to say, back at the house. A kiss won't be enough. Things aren't going to stop there with us."

"Where will they stop, Morgan?"

He shook his head. "Only you can decide that, because my answer might not be the one you want to hear."

She knew then that what he was really saying was that he could make her no promises beyond today, and that she had to determine if she could live with the fact, afterward, when this special place in time was no more than a memory and they had gone their separate ways.

Why did this have to be so complicated? she wondered, shifting her gaze to the silent, watchful trees. Why couldn't love between a man and a woman be straightforward and mutual, instead of plagued by self-doubt and the insecurity of never knowing for sure the depth of the other person's feelings?

She had thought, when Stuart had filled every corner of her life, that what she'd shared with him was extraordinary, and strong enough to withstand whatever test was flung in its path. But at the end of it all what she'd mistaken for love had turned out to be nothing but an illusion.

"Not that we haven't had fun," he'd told her with charming regret, the day he'd decided she was becoming too much of a liability, "but I can't afford to run the risk of getting fired from this job."

"Fired?" She'd stared at him, too stunned—too *stupid*—to comprehend where the conversation was leading. "We can't be fired for falling in love, Stuart!"

"Ah, well," he'd said, running a paint-stained fingertip down her cheek, "if that were all, perhaps not."

Premonition had cast a chilling shadow over her at his words. "It's all that matters to me," she'd cried, turning her cheek and pressing her mouth to his palm in a desperate kiss. He'd been cleaning the brushes used by his senior oil-painting class and even now, five years later, the smell of turpentine revived the memory of that day in stark and degrading detail. "Nothing else compares."

He'd snatched his hand away and cast a nervous eye at the glass-paned door of the art room, as if afraid a passing student or teacher might happen to glance in and see what was taking place. "But we haven't been as discreet as we hoped. It seems we were spotted together away from the school and the sort of gossip that's given rise to, well...." He'd backed away and his lopsided, careless smile had torn her heart to shreds. "The fact of the matter is, I'm married, sweet thing, and damn me if I don't like the arrangement."

So many little things she'd refused to acknowledge had risen up to confront her then. The fact that they spent almost all their time in the shuttered privacy of her apartment. He seldom took her out in public and when he did it was to some obscure little hole in the wall at the other end of town, or, better yet, out of town altogether.

The fact that they never shared special times like Christmas. "Must pay my respects to the family," he'd say, with such dutiful long-suffering that she'd overflowed with sympathy for him, even though she would have given everything she possessed to have a family of her own to go home to. "Terribly tedious, of course, and I wouldn't dream of asking you to traipse halfway across the continent with me. You'd be bored out of your skull, darling. Best you do your thing and I'll do mine, and we'll make up for it in the new year."

And, perhaps most telling of all, his insistence that they keep their relationship secret from their co-workers. "It's not a good idea to try to mix work with pleasure," he'd said, the first time they'd made love. "Let that lot of busybodies think we're just friendly colleagues. They'll have a field day discussing us if they ever find out differently."

But the other teachers had talked anyway. If their sudden silences when she walked into the staffroom hadn't told her so, their pitying glances had. She'd thought it was because he was so much older than she was, and had turned a deaf ear when a few of the younger staff had tried to involve her in their own social groups. Only when he'd dropped the news that he was married had she understood that they'd known all along what was going on and had felt sorry for her.

She had not been able to bear the humiliation. The day after the affair ended, she'd gone to her school principal and asked for a transfer. He'd agreed to arrange it at once. "I wish you'd come to me months ago," he'd said sadly.

And now there was Morgan, not married by all accounts, but just as much of a threat in his way. What about all the things she didn't know about him, things she sensed but which he would not divulge?

But what about the things you do know? her foolish heart cried. Don't they count? He's decent and kind and responsible. He took you in, gave you a place to stay, made you feel at home. And he's brought you back to life, in places no one else can see. You've learned to feel again since he came into your life, to want. To *ache*, deep inside, to *melt*.

Helpless to deny any of it, she flicked her gaze back to his and read the same charged awareness in his eyes.

"Jessica?"

Compellingly quiet, his voice rolled over her, like vintage port, deep and dark. Like smoky autumn days and rich auburn sunsets. Like love....

Love? her scandalized brain scoffed. Be sensible, for pity's sake. What can love possibly have to do with this?

Perhaps nothing, but the magnetism or whatever it was drummed a swift percussion in her blood, leaving her surely a little insane. Because what she actually did was lean into him and put her arms around his waist so that not a breath of the clear, cold air could come between them, and say, "I think we should stop worrying about tomorrow and concentrate on how we feel tonight."

His breath caught in his throat. "You're sure?"

She nodded. That was all but it was enough.

Dipping his head, he fastened his lips to hers to seal the contract and let them remain there as his feet retraced a path to the shore. Her body moved smoothly with his, the uncertainty gone, the outcome assured.

His lips tasted of cold and snow and frosty starlight. Of passion barely leashed, of scorching hunger and fiery need. Out there on the ice, with the rest of the world paralyzed in winter's iron grip, what had begun as a candle's flicker of attraction burst into flames and all that mattered was that the waiting was over. Right or wrong, wise or not, she and Morgan had made a choice and there was no going back.

Finally, he wrestled his mouth away from hers and took her by the arm. Urgently, silently, he steered her along the path under the trees, back toward the house. Once he stopped and, pressing her up against the trunk of a cedar, took her face in his gloved hands and kissed her again, as though to reaffirm their decision, to stoke the fire lest it die before they had the chance to warm themselves at its flame.

His tongue spoke impassioned volumes, echoing the urgent thrust of his body against hers. Weak at the knees and utterly breathless, she thought for a moment that they'd never make it back to the house, that he'd take her out there in the shadows, with the snow for a mattress and the stars for a cover.

He didn't. He released her, grasped her arm again and, in a voice rough with passion, muttered, "For Pete's sake, let's get back to the house before I lose what little sanity I have left."

CHAPTER EIGHT

THE magic held, speeding them back across the frozen snow, fleet-footed and giddy with hunger for each other. Once inside the house, Morgan shucked off his boots, helped Jessica get rid of hers, peeled her free of the heavy down jacket and flung it with his across the newel post.

"You've got cold hands," he said, chafing them between his.

And I'm getting cold feet, she thought miserably, the practicalities of what they were about to enter into filling her with misgivings.

He'd probably want to strip her naked. He'd see how plain she was then, how straight up and down except for her unremarkable little breasts. Men liked breasts on a woman—lush, ripe, big breasts. Men liked fire in a woman—unbridled passion and a sense of adventure.

Whatever had made her think she could please him?

He dropped a kiss on her mouth and, winding an arm around her waist, led her upstairs. She allowed him to because she couldn't resist. His touch, his kiss, the heated glances he sent her way brought out a lust in her she'd never suspected.

Lust? Her romantic heart rebelled. *Lust wasn't what this was all about!*

What else would you like to call it, dear? the eminently down-to-earth Miss Simms, the headmistress, inquired loftily.

Still she could not free herself of his spell. Blushing, she allowed him to draw her over the threshold to his room. She'd never been inside before. Even during the day the door had always been closed and, curious though she'd been, she hadn't seen it as her right to snoop. He kicked it closed behind them now and flicked on a reading lamp that filled the shadows with too much light.

Like the room itself, his bed, she saw at once, was huge—a marriage bed, plenty big enough for two. And nothing between them and it except a few yards of carpet. She averted her eyes and wished he hadn't turned on the lamp.

Apart from a tall armoire, a set of drawers and two bedside tables, the rest of the room was bare. Short of climbing into the wardrobe, there was no place to which a person might retire to undress discreetly. And she had so many layers of clothes to shed, not the least of which was the long red underwear.

A wave of color swept over her face at the thought of him seeing her in *that*!

"Jessica," he said, linking his fingers through hers and watching her closely, "are you having second thoughts?"

Of course she was! She had absolutely no business contemplating making love with a man she'd known less than a week and, if she were honest, she'd come straight out and tell him she was afraid. But the plainer truth was that, despite the eleventh-hour attack of nerves, her body and soul cried out for him with a fine disregard for moral convention, and she was damned if she was going to turn away from him just because old fears had risen up to haunt her.

"You are very sweet," Stuart had told her, that day he'd shut the door on their affair, "but not exactly a challenge any more, my dear, if you know what I mean."

She'd known only too well. For him, the thrill had been in the chase, in being the first to seduce her. Once he'd accomplished that, he was ready to go on to other conquests.

Well, she had no virginity to lose now, no illusions to shatter. All she had—might ever have—was this moment and Morgan, and the miracle of his wanting her with the same urgency that she craved him. It showed in the molten glow of his eyes, in his clenched jaw, in the tension that held him immobile as he waited for her reply.

"I'm not having second thoughts," she assured him. "I—"

"Because if you are," he went on, "we can stop right now. I won't think badly of you for changing your mind, but—"

"This is what I want," she insisted quickly, before fear that she might disappoint him had her running for the hills.

He laid a finger across her lips. "But I will think very badly of myself if, tomorrow, you decide you've made a horrible mistake."

Out there on the frozen lake she had felt free and strong enough to let her secret self emerge, enough to dare let the romantic in her run free, even if it was only for tonight. She wasn't stupid; she knew her real life was drawn along different, more realistic lines, but just for this one special night she'd come to believe in miracles.

He had made that possible with his kisses and the way he'd looked at her. And now, with his probing questions, he was threatening to take it away. He was resurrecting the headmistress who never acted without due consideration, who never gave in to wild impulses. She didn't want to be that woman. Not here, not now.

"You're trying to talk me out of it, aren't you?" she cried, flinching a little. "Why? Because you've changed *your* mind?"

He slid his hands around her neck, lacing his fingers at her nape and stroking his thumbs along her cheekbones. "No," he said hoarsely. "Right or wrong, I've wanted you practically from the moment I first laid eyes on you. But I'm not sure you...."

"What?" she said, tilting her head so that his hand was captured between her jaw and her shoulder. *"What?"*

He hesitated, his gaze scouring her face. "I'm wondering how much...if this is the first—"

Sweet heaven, he was afraid he was going to rob her of her innocence and that she'd expect him to compensate by making an honest woman of her! "You think I'm some naive, terrified virgin, don't you? But I'm not—a virgin, I mean. I had an affair once...." She drew a sharp, defiant breath. "With a married man."

But he continued to study her with cool dispassion and saw that she'd told only half the truth. "You didn't know he was married at the time, though, did you?"

His insight punctured her bravado, leaving her feeling almost as big a fool as she had the day she'd found out Stuart had been toying with her all along. "No," she whispered miserably. "If I had, I never would have gotten involved with him."

"Well," he murmured, drawing a tender fingertip down her throat with potent effect, "I've already told you I'm not married. That much, at least, I can promise you."

It was, at best, a conditional vow but at least it was honest. And what else could he say? That he loved her? If he had, she wouldn't have believed him. Rational people didn't fall in love in a matter of days and if the realization tore at her heart a little it was because she'd been starving for romance for so long that it was difficult not to want the whole package.

"You don't have to promise me anything," she said, running her hands over the solid planes of his chest. "We haven't known each other long enough to make those kinds of demands on each other. But even if I never see you again after I leave this house I will treasure the memories I take away with me. Let what we share tonight be a Christmas gift each of us gives freely to the other.''

Oh, she mourned, hearing the teacher in her upstage the lover, what a pompous idiot he must think I am!

But an expression touched his features then that she couldn't decipher, a spasm of near-grief, almost. He took her face in his two hands and looked so deeply into her eyes that he might have been searching for her soul. Beneath her hand, his heart thumped unevenly. ''Where were you when I was young and optimistic, Jessica Simms?'' he murmured, inching his mouth toward hers. ''And what have I done to deserve you now?''

By design or happy accident—she neither knew nor cared which—his kiss swept them past the awkwardness and recaptured the passion. Suddenly, his hands were everywhere, urging her toward the bed and undressing her every step of the way, layer by layer even to the abominable red underwear, until all that covered her were her satin camisole, bra and panties.

As if she'd caught his fever, her own hands deployed themselves with shameful abandon, tugging, sliding, stripping him too—not quite as expertly as he'd stripped her, perhaps, but with every bit as much fervor.

A trail of clothing marked their haste, her camisole at last slithering beneath his briefs, her bra hooking immodestly into the opening of his cords as they fell to the floor.

Breathless, eager, anxious, she felt the edge of the bed hit the back of her knees and sank to the mattress. He stood before her, naked and indecently gorgeous in the lamplight.

And then he was beside her, the scent of him—his skin, his hair—swamping her senses. The warmth of his big male body next to hers, the probing sensitivity of his hands as they discovered her, the dedication with which he readied her to accept him turned her to liquid fire.

But what made her love him was his gentleness, and his patience. Because for all that she wanted him so badly, she first had to overcome the knot of inhibition that held her hostage—a paralyzing relic of self-doubt, courtesy of the only other man she'd known, which allowed her to participate just so far and then no further.

Morgan sensed it and set about releasing her with an insight that moved her to tears.

At delicious, excruciating leisure, he kissed her fingertips, her throat, the soft skin of her inner elbow. He stroked her face, her shoulder, traced a line between her breasts and down her ribs, smoothed his hand over her hips and up her thigh.

And thus, by degrees so slight she barely noticed their progress, he sought her most intimate flesh, all the time murmuring words in her ear, calling her sweetheart, telling her she was beautiful.

And at that moment she believed him. She felt beautiful—voluptuously female and beautiful and desirable. Enough that she dared touch him, too, cradling the heat of him, marveling at the silken strength of him, and near melting with the need to feel him buried deep inside her.

But he had further exquisite torture to inflict. Like ripples in a pond, his touch aroused ever widening rings of awareness within her until, suddenly, she broke free of all restraint and exploded into arching spasms of response. The havoc they created to her equilibrium was purely indescribable.

Only then, when she lay quivering with pleasure and calling out his name in a throaty murmur, did he come to her. Not hastily or covertly, but with a smooth, sure power that allowed for no regrets, just soaring elation and a shimmering suspension that she never wanted to end.

He held her close, rocked within her, introduced her to an intimacy she'd never known before. It was enough. More than enough. Closing her hands over his shoulders, she thought dimly that she would remember him and this night for the rest of her life.

But he had not done giving. "Stay with me," he whispered against her mouth, sliding his hands beneath her hips and lifting her to meet his suddenly accelerated rhythm.

She gasped at the deeper invasion, fought the old demons again as they rose up to hinder her, but they had lost their power. The confines of her existence shifted, broadened; a new horizon beckoned, and they were together, she and Morgan, riding blindly toward a destination as unavoidable as it was terrifying and exhilarating.

Her hands convulsed, her nails dug into the solid muscle of his shoulders, gouged frantically at his back. She heard a whimpering, a cry that echoed from somewhere beyond eternity, and realized it had come from her.

He answered her and for one endless, trembling moment held them both suspended. In spiraling slow motion, she felt herself expand beyond anything mortal or earthly, felt her heart fuse with his, felt her body aching and yearning and reaching…reaching….

The shattering of release, when it came, fractured her soul.

For a few, passion-drenched minutes, she lay beneath him, too saturated with emotion to move. Slowly, the separate parts of her assumed their separate identities again, though not quite as they had been before—she'd never again be that person! But the mind began to function, the knowledge to unwind.

Wrapping her arms tightly around him, she buried her face in his neck to stop herself from saying out loud that she loved him. Because at that moment, with the memory of his possession still echoing in her blood, she did love him. But she knew that if she told him so she would ruin the perfection of what they'd shared because it was the last thing he wanted to hear.

For a while longer, he remained with his big body covering hers, unmoving except for the diminishing thunder of his heart against her breast. Finally, he rolled to his side and took her with him.

His hair lay damp against his forehead, his skin, still lightly tanned from summer, gleamed. His eyes had the sated, sleepy look of a man well pleased with the woman in his arms. He had never been more handsome, never more charming.

"Well," he said, pinning her securely in his arms and smiling down at her, "what can I say?"

Coming up with an answer was worse than picking her way through a minefield. "Merry Christmas?" she ventured.

She heard the laughter rumble deep within his chest. "And then some! Jessica Simms, you are quite exceptional and I hope you know that."

But not so exceptional that he could say the words drumming repeatedly in her head. *I love you, even if it is just for tonight.*

Alarmed at the turn her thoughts persisted in taking, she wriggled away from him. How had such a notion managed to creep up on her? Falling in love with a man simply because he'd taken her to bed was a cliché that went out of date in the sixties, one only slightly less absurd than expecting him to reciprocate the sentiment.

"Hey," he said, making a grab for her, "where do you think you're going?"

"Back to my own room," she replied, neatly evading him and swathing herself in the duvet. Never mind that that left him with only a sheet to keep himself warm; she could no more face the prospect of walking out of his room stark naked, feeling his eyes track her every step, than she could remain there and keep her shocking secret to herself. Another minute and he'd see it written on her face, even if she managed to keep her mouth shut. Darn him for turning on that lamp, anyway!

"Why?" he said. "What's wrong with staying here?"

"What would Clancy think, if he knew?"

"Hang Clancy! This is about you and me."

"Nevertheless," she said primly, "I don't care to advertise my private life and I don't imagine you do, either."

Shoving himself up onto one elbow, he watched her, and if she hadn't known better she'd have thought he looked a little hurt at her sudden defection. "True, but that's no reason for you to race off in such a hurry now without so much as a goodnight kiss." Not the least abashed by the fact that the sheet had slipped to reveal more of him than it covered, he beckoned her with the forefinger of his other hand. "Come back here, Jessica. It's not as if I'm expecting company in the next—"

He'd been about to go on cajoling her in the same light-hearted vein. She heard it in his voice, saw it in his lazy, slightly wicked smile. But all at once he bit off the words and flopped onto his back with a scowl. "On the other hand," he finished, one of his sudden mood swings taking hold and souring the moment, "perhaps you're right. Perhaps we are better off in separate beds."

"Exactly." Turning away from him, she stopped to collect her scattered clothing. He must not see the sudden sparkle of tears she dared not blink away for fear they'd splash down her face and betray her.

Good, sound common sense was all very fine, but bringing it to bear on the situation so lamentably after the fact served no purpose at all beyond reminding her that she was a fool and him that she was a temporary diversion.

"Well," she said, making tracks for the door and amazed that her voice sounded so thoroughly normal, "goodnight, Morgan. I'll see you in the morning."

"Jessica?" he said, in a low voice.

She stopped with her hand on the knob but didn't turn. She didn't think she could bear to look on his sleek, male beauty again that night and not grovel at his feet. "Yes?"

"Merry Christmas. It really was special tonight."

It's not as if I'm expecting company...

Morgan lay flat on his back in the dark, cursing himself and the careless utterance that had stripped the evening of its magic and left him staring into the ugly face of the reality waiting for him, if not tomorrow, then the next day or the day after that.

How could he have forgotten it, even for a moment? How could he have allowed himself, besotted imbecile that he was, to become so drawn into the web of attraction she'd spun about him that he'd risked her safety, too?

He should have listened to his first instinct and left her to fend for herself when they'd been rescued from the avalanche shed. Failing that, he should have listened to Clancy and refused to let her remain in the house. She'd have been safer bunking down on a bench at Stedman's service station than here with him.

The damnable thing was, it was too late. A lot too late. No use telling himself he'd known her only three days. Time was relative when emotions interfered. And after tonight it might as well have been a lifetime, because he and Jessica had connected—connected in a way he'd never experienced with Daphne whom he'd known for nearly three years before he'd married her.

A rising wind moaned low around the house. Indication of another blizzard, perhaps, one that would keep Jessica safe prisoner here another few days? What the hell good would that do, beyond strengthening the bond he'd had no business forging in the first place?

Morgan sighed and reached for the illuminated dial of his watch on the bedside table. Almost three in the morning. Another five hours and it would be daylight. Christmas Day in the high country. And somewhere out there

Gabriel Parrish waited while, across the hall, Jessica lay alone in her bed.

Cursing again, he sat up and bunched the pillows behind his head and accepted what he could no longer deny. Things had progressed far beyond the point of his offering a stranger the kindness of a roof over her head until the weather improved. He wanted to keep her with him, explore the wider possibilities of the relationship that had sprung up between them. He wanted to protect her, to preserve her air of unsullied purity, her innocence.

"You want to take on the whole damned world," his ex-wife had accused him bitterly during one of their endless fights about his work, and in a way she'd been right. He *had* been too busy fighting other people's battles to take proper care of his marriage.

But this went beyond the ordinary range of things and had nothing to do with his commitment to sweeping society clean of its human filth. Jessica touched his heart and made him want to rush out and slay dragons for her, a dangerously quixotic fancy that he could ill afford with the very real threat of Gabriel Parrish hovering.

Jessica was precisely Parrish's kind of victim: fragile, vulnerable, gentle. And far from protecting her Morgan had put her smack in the path of danger.

Of course, he could explain the whole mess to her and hope she'd understand. And then what? Have her cringe every time a twig snapped in the cold? Have her looking over her shoulder the whole time she was alone in his house? Have her despise him more than she already did?

Because it was obvious that was how she felt and she'd wasted no time letting him know it, after the loving. If he hadn't heard her cries, felt the helpless contractions of her flesh around his, he'd have thought he'd lost his touch. But just as there'd been no mistaking her climactic response there'd been no mistaking the haste with which she'd departed the scene, once she'd recovered herself, and no misreading the rejection in the erect line of her spine as she'd stood at the door and bid him a cool goodnight.

Thank you for a pleasant interlude, Mr. Kincaid, but now that it's over I see very little reason to prolong the evening.

He'd known a violent urge to argue the point, an unprecedented occurrence for him. He didn't chase after reluctant women; they weren't worth the effort, not when so many others were willing. And heaven could attest to the fact that he wasn't in the market for a long-term affair. Nor, for that matter, was she. A brief encounter they could handle. A dalliance. Something that wouldn't scratch below the surface of their separate lives.

A waltz with a stranger—lilting, briefly and engagingly intimate—but no more permanent than the ice on the frozen lake.

When had the rules changed for him?

A sound penetrated the silence, a creaking that was probably nothing more than the house settling its old bones into the winter night, but which could equally well be a stealthy footfall announcing the arrival of an intruder.

Morgan raked exasperated fingers through his hair. For crying out loud, that was all he needed: to have his imagination run any wilder than it already was!

But once planted the suspicion refused to die. What if Parrish had tracked him down despite the weather and was even now inside the house, searching for his archenemy? What if he opened the wrong door by mistake and discovered Jessica?

Cold sweat broke out along Morgan's spine.

Flinging back the covers, he swung out of bed and pulled on his robe, his feet silent on the floor. Cautiously, he inched open his door.

Nothing. No darting, furtive shadow, no sense of evil

lurking, just the quiet hum of the oil furnace and the dim fragrance of the Christmas tree stealing up the stairs.

Across the hall, the door to Jessica's room stood closed. Was she inside, safely sleeping, or had the sound that had alerted him wakened her, too? His outstretched hand froze mere inches from the doorknob.

Hell, Kincaid, he jeered silently, who're you trying to fool? You're just itching to find a reason to go in there and pretending there's a bogeyman haunting the place is about as feeble an excuse as you can get.

But what if...? The spectre of Parrish rose again to haunt him. Grasping the knob, he quietly opened her door and stepped into the room.

Moonlight splashed across the floor and over the bed. She lay in the middle of the mattress, so straight and still that for one wild, irrational moment he wondered if he'd left it too late, wondered if Parrish had found her and she was already dead. And then she turned her head and he saw that her eyes were wide open and watching him.

"Morgan?" Her voice swam across to him, soft, misty, full of yearning. Like her eyes as they tracked his progress toward the bed.

She held out her arms, silvered with moonlight, and with that simple, eloquent gesture flattened any hope he'd entertained of staying away from her. He could love this woman, he realized despairingly. Love her in ways he hadn't known how to love when he'd married Daphne.

With a muffled groan, he swept aside the covers and strode back to his room, cradling her next to his heart.

They fell on the bed together, mouths devouring each other, hands tormenting, limbs tangling. She was hot and damp and sleekly alluring. Their mating was swift and too frantic to allow for any pretense at finesse or responsibility.

Her body welcomed him, closed around him, caressed

him. In vain he tried to hold back, to distance himself just enough to prolong the pleasure for both of them, but it was too late. Without warning she climaxed in a flight of ripples that had him flooding within her in shocking, sudden release.

She was so ready to love, he thought sadly, cradling her sleeping body. So ready to *be* loved. Why had it been he who'd found her? Why not some man whose soul was intact, whose heart had not grown black and bitter, whose energies were bent on something other than a crusade that left him with so little to offer a woman?

Jessica didn't awake until nine on Christmas morning, and even then she might have slept another hour had the sun not crept through the window to shine full on her face.

She was alone in the bed with only the faint warmth where Morgan had lain beside her as proof that she hadn't dreamed the night before. That and her pleasurably aching body.

By the time she was showered and dressed, any hope she'd entertained of trying to pretend this morning was no different from the others she'd spent at the lodge had evaporated. The men were back at the house already, their early chores at the stables completed. "O Come All Ye Faithful" floated up the stairs from the old record player in the living room, along with the smell of frying food from the kitchen.

Securing her hair in its usual smooth loop at her nape, Jessica took a deep, calming breath and prepared to face Morgan, wishing that she could have done so without Clancy there as witness.

It was a far worse experience than she'd anticipated. Morgan sat at the kitchen table, his hands wrapped around his coffee mug. Clancy stood at the stove, swishing something around in the large, cast-iron frying pan, and it was clear from the scowl he shot her way that he'd deployed the last of his Christmas spirit the night before.

"Well, lookee what the cat drug down," he declared evilly.

Jessica resisted the urge to fidget with the collar of her blouse. "I'm afraid I overslept."

"Do tell." He shoveled the contents of the frying pan onto three plates and slapped one down in front of her.

She looked at the greasy mess and swallowed. Chunks of ham floated among half-cooked eggs, alongside hash-browned potatoes swimming in a sea of grease.

Looking up, she found Morgan studying her. "Good morning," he said, a faintly conspiratorial smile warming his eyes. "I hope you're hungry."

Sweet heaven, yes—but not for what stared up from her plate! Picking up her fork, Jessica speared a morsel of ham that glistened with fat. "Not very," she said, suppressing a delicate shudder. "I think I'll just have toast."

"Ain't made toast, and idlers can't be choosers," Clancy informed her sourly. "You choose to lollygag in bed when any decent, self-respectin' woman'd be at the kitchen stove where she rightly belongs, then you put up with what lands on your plate or else go hungry."

"That's enough, Clancy," Morgan warned quietly, keeping his gaze trained on her. "Jessica doesn't need your permission to sleep in. I wasn't up at the crack of dawn myself."

Clancy flicked a knowing glance from her to Morgan and back again. "Hah! Ain't that a coincidence and a half!"

Jessica felt a slow burn climb up her neck to inflame her face and wished she could fall through a crack in the floor. "Well," she said, deciding this was not the time to take issue with Clancy's chauvinistic views on women and their rightful role in society, "I'm sure this is delicious, whatever it is."

And to prove the point she valiantly scooped a forkful into her mouth. Across the table, Morgan continued to watch her, his hands still wrapped around his coffee mug.

Memories floated over, of those same hands covering her breasts, measuring her waist, parting her thighs, still-ing her eager hips. "I don't understand myself," she'd confessed, pressing herself to him and reveling in the knowledge that, regardless of what he might be trying to tell her, a certain portion of his own anatomy had an actively rebellious mind of its own. "It's as if I've got an attack of polar fever or something."

"Or something." His words had slid into her mouth along with his tongue, wreaking delicious devastation.

She'd felt her barriers disintegrating again, melted by the moist heat swirling the length of her and flooding warmly against him, there, in that most private place that he'd touched and stroked and incited to ecstasy.

How embarrassing to remember it now! How shame-less!

The color flooded her face anew, so fiercely that it wouldn't have surprised her too greatly to find her fore-head emblazoned with a large scarlet WH for Wanton Hussy.

The food in her mouth rebelled furiously and threat-ened to choke her. Morgan pushed back his chair, picked up her plate, scraped the contents into the garbage can under the sink, then popped two slices of bread in the toaster.

"Coffee?" he asked her, lifting the coffee pot from its spot on top of the woodstove.

She nodded gratefully. "Thank you."

"How about you, Clancy? Ready for a refill?"

Eyes darting observantly back and forth, Clancy grunted acceptance.

Morgan topped up his own mug, too, replaced the pot on the stove and, leaning his hips against the counter, drummed a soft tattoo on the back of his chair as he waited for the toast to brown.

Covertly, Jessica studied him. He had the tall, sculpted build of a telemark skier, she thought dreamily. Sharply defined, clear-eyed. Sexy. She leaned toward him, drinking in the sharp, clean fragrance of him.

The toast sprang up, startling her. Morgan turned to attend to it.

"Lordy, woman," Clancy drawled, sotto voce, "eat him up whole, why don'tcha?"

"Here's your toast," Morgan said, placing a fresh plate in front of her. "Hurry up and eat, then get your coat. I've got a surprise waiting outside."

CHAPTER NINE

As CURIOUS to discover what Morgan had in store for her as she was eager to escape Clancy's too observant eye, Jessica literally bolted through her breakfast. Nothing, however, could have prepared her for the sight that met her eyes when she stepped out onto the front veranda.

At the foot of the steps stood a sleek red sleigh with a high padded seat clearing the runners by a good two feet. Jasper waited patiently between twin wooden shafts, silver bells gleaming from his harness.

"Thought you might like to go for a spin," Morgan said, coming up beside her. "You've been kind of housebound lately."

"Yes." Jessica stood transfixed, as thrilled as a child. "Morgan, what an absolutely gorgeous sleigh!"

"Isn't it?" He stroked a proud hand over the painted side and swung open the little door. "Hop aboard and let's get going while the sun's still high."

She climbed up the two narrow steps and settled into the red leather seat. There were hot bricks wrapped in flannel for her feet and a marvellous fur lap rug to keep the chill out.

"Buffalo robes," Morgan explained, when she asked. "Guaranteed to cut the wind, no matter how cold it gets."

He climbed up beside her, gathered up the reins and clicked his tongue, a signal that had Jasper moving over the snowed-in driveway to the open country beyond.

The scene unrolled like something from *Dr. Zhivago*. Seated beside Morgan, her face framed by the fur-trimmed hood of her jacket, her knees covered by buffalo robes, her feet toasting gently on the hot bricks, Jessica gazed around, eager not to miss a thing as they followed a course along the ridge to the west of the house.

To either side the land dropped away, remote and empty save for the occasional group of snow-laden trees. Ahead, the razor-backed mountains reared up, their winter load dazzling against the deep blue sky.

Except for the soft squeak of the sleigh runners and the jingle of bells on Jasper's harness, the silence was profound to the point of being almost somnolent.

"That married man you mentioned," Morgan said suddenly, the sound of his voice flowing into the still air as smoothly as the hot rum sauce had rolled over the ice cream dessert she'd made the night before, "the one you had the affair with, were you in love with him?"

"Stuart?" Jessica blinked. What had Stuart to do with anything? "Yes. I was very hurt when he ended things between us."

"And now?"

She flung Morgan a questioning stare and found him concentrating fiercely on his driving. "Now?"

His glance flicked briefly over her, then focused on the scene ahead again. "Do you still care about him?"

"No!" she exclaimed. "If I did, I'd never have made love with you last night."

"The two don't necessarily cancel each other out, you know."

"They do for me. I'm not the type to play musical beds." She paused and hazarded another sidelong glance at him. His profile was almost as remote as the countryside. "Are you trying to tell me you are, Morgan?"

"No." He hauled on the reins and brought Jasper to a halt in the lee of a belt of trees. "I like to be able to live with myself the morning after."

The easy relaxation between them when they'd first started out seeped away suddenly, leaving behind a tension as fragile as crystal shimmering in the bright white sunshine. "Then why did you bring up the subject in the first place?"

He sighed and leaned forward to rest his elbows on his knees. "I guess I'm wondering where we go from here. Yesterday, I thought I knew. Today, I'm not so sure."

It was an admission that might have charged her with elation had the darkness in his tone not indicated such a wealth of regret on his part for the fact that they'd made love.

"Well," she said, rushing to fill the silence with an admission more easily borne coming out of her mouth than his, "what happened between us...well, it was a purely physical thing—at least for me."

"Was it?" She could feel his gaze boring into her, seeking to discover truth and fearing, quite rightly, that he'd find only lies. "Then why do I feel like pond scum this morning? As if I've let both of us down and hurt you in the bargain?"

"You haven't hurt me," she said staunchly, because the other option, to burst out crying for something he clearly couldn't give her, would be more humiliation than she could abide. "You've been honest with me and that's what matters."

Broodingly, he studied the distant valley. "Honesty's very important to you, isn't it, Jessica?"

"Yes, especially where feelings are concerned. I lived with the lie of my aunt's supposed affection for years, even though she tried hard not to let it show that she really didn't care much for me."

She drew in a deep breath of the crisp air and prayed it would dispel the sudden urge to bare her soul to him. Wallowing in self-pity was unattractive at the best of times and always dangerous. She no more wanted his pity than she did his affectations of love. She'd endured enough of both to last her a lifetime. "I think there is nothing more insulting than to be the recipient of that sort of deceit."

"Were you very young when you went to live with her?"

"Yes." Jessica pushed back the jacket hood and lifted her face to the pale winter sun. "I was eight at the time and Selena was five. Of course, I had no idea how my aunt felt about taking us in."

"How long before you found out?"

"Quite some time." Jessica plucked at the fur robe covering her lap. "In her way, she tried very hard to be a good substitute parent, but it was more a question of noblesse oblige than real affection. She and my uncle had elected not to have a family of their own and I think suddenly finding herself stuck with someone else's small, unhappy children cramped her style terribly."

"At least you and your sister had each other." He took off his gloves and spread one arm along the high cushioned backrest of the seat. "No wonder you were so anxious to get to her when you heard about her accident. You must be very close."

"Not really. As we grew older, we found we had very little in common." She shrugged, burningly conscious of his hand draped over her shoulder. "Selena adapted to her new situation much better than I did. My aunt was a real society matron—gave lots of smart, expensive parties at which she liked to have us put in an appearance so that everyone could commend her for the wonderful thing she was doing. I was a plain, shy child with no social graces at all, but Selena was a party animal from the word go. Pretty, entertaining, amusing. A very easy child to love, even if she didn't have my feet."

"Your feet?" Morgan turned toward her and let out a bark of surprised laughter. "What the hell have your feet got to do with anything?"

"They're my finest feature," Jessica said candidly. "Apart from my brains, they're the *only* feature I have that's worth mentioning, if my aunt is to be believed."

"Then your aunt is a damn fool," he told her, "and so are you if you believe that sort of rubbish."

"She did her best in a difficult situation. You have to understand that Selena barely remembered our parents but I did, and I missed them horribly. I didn't want someone else trying to take their place. I wasn't affectionate or...or giving, like Selena. She'd hand out kisses and hugs indiscriminately and loved to be dressed up like a doll and paraded before other people, whereas I was...."

"Yes?" His hand strayed up to stroke her cheek. "What were you, Jessica?"

"Ungrateful, probably. Standoffish, certainly." She gave the buffalo robe an irritable twitch, annoyed to hear a faint whine of self-pity in her voice despite her best efforts to prevent it. "How many poor animals died to make this, do you suppose?"

If he was surprised at the sudden change of topic, he didn't show it. "I've no idea. It was something my great-grandfather gave to my great-grandmother the same year he had this cutter made for her." Swinging sideways on the seat, Morgan brought his other hand over and covered Jessica's, capturing it next to the robe and leaving her trapped in the loose circle of his arms. "Until then, people around here thought she was standoffish, too."

How was it possible that, with winter all around them, just his touch could leave her flushed with rosy warmth? Studiously avoiding his gaze and certain he must be able to hear the uneven thumping of her heart in the silence, Jessica said, "And was she?"

"No. Like you, she was simply different. Born in England, one of four children, affluent parents, private governess, debutante, the whole society nine yards. When the First World War broke out, she became a nurse and went to work in a hospital in London. She fell in love with my great-grandfather when he was shipped there to recover from wounds he suffered in France. They were married in 1918, a big society wedding at her family's country estate, and he brought her home to Canada right after that."

"Home being here, at the house?" So drawn in by the story that she forgot to worry about the effect of how close Morgan was sitting or how snugly his arm had closed around her shoulder, Jessica swung around to face him.

"Not quite. He built the lodge over the next several years. To begin with, they lived in a cabin with no running water or indoor plumbing."

"Good grief, talk about culture shock!"

"Exactly." Morgan nodded. "My great-grandmother was homesick and lonely. She gave birth to her first child, my grandmother, in that cabin, with no one to help her, no relatives to fuss over her, none of the comforts she'd been brought up to expect. She had nothing in common with other wives in the area and no friends. Her only contact with the outside world came through the letters she received from home and by the time they arrived the news they contained was months old. Her entire life took place within those four walls with her baby and my great-grandfather who, during the summer especially, spent nearly every waking hour working the ranch."

"She must have loved him very much."

"She did, but even so the marriage almost fell apart when her second baby was stillborn. She was alone at the time and was convinced the child could have been saved had there been someone there to help her."

"I cannot imagine the pain that must have brought her, to lose a child."

"It's not something I would wish on my worst enemy," Morgan said, with such feeling that, if he hadn't already told her there'd been no children, Jessica would have wondered if he and his wife had lost a son or daughter.

"What saved the marriage?" she asked, as much to alleviate the sudden darkening of his mood as to hear the rest of the story.

"She told him she was going home again and taking

their surviving child with her, because she couldn't stand the isolation a day longer. Her son lay buried within sight of the house and her daughter was growing up a prisoner of the wilderness, learning none of the social graces that would have been part of her life if she'd grown up in England.''

Jessica studied Morgan's profile and thought that, if the old man had been one iota as handsome or one tenth as skilled a lover as his great-grandson, no woman could have walked away from him. ''But he talked her out of it?''

''No, he hitched the horse to the buggy, drove her into town and bought her a ticket so that she could catch the next train heading east. But when it came right down to it she couldn't leave him. She had her bags on the train and one foot on the step, ready to climb into the carriage, and then made the mistake of looking down into his big, dumb face, and supposedly said, 'After everything we've been through together, are you just going to stand there and let me walk out of your life, you stupid fool?'''

''Oh,'' Jessica said, blinking furiously as the silly tears threatened, ''I've always been a pushover for happy endings.''

''Well,'' Morgan said, his eyes scouring her face, ''it didn't quite end there. Of course, she came back here with him, but the shock of what had almost happened made them take stock. They both realized she needed contact with other people, and a purpose beyond simply being a wife and mother. So, that Christmas, he presented her with the cutter, and she started visiting the other ranchers' wives. Before long, word got around that she'd been a nurse and the next thing she was being called on to help deliver babies, and by the following summer, when the foundations for the house were being built, she'd become something of a legend up here.''

He paused for breath and grinned at her. ''What was your original question again, Jessica?''

"I asked about the buffalo robe."

"Ah, yes. Well, now you know."

"So tell me the rest."

"There's not much to tell. My grandmother went away to school but came home one summer and fell in love with a neighboring rancher. They married and had only one child, my father. He moved to the coast when he went to university, met my mother there, and settled in Vancouver where I was born. The ranch dwindled, with some of the land eventually being sold off after my grandparents died, and the property lay more or less neglected until I took an interest in it."

"And your sister?" Jessica asked. "You haven't mentioned her except in passing."

"She married a Frenchman and lives in Marseilles. We keep in touch, of course, but we're not close the way we once were."

Jessica turned her hand palm up so that her fingers curved around his. "I'm sorry, Morgan."

"Yeah, well...." He blew out a long breath that curled foggily in the still air. "I guess that happens when another man enters a woman's life."

"That must hurt. Selena can be a pain at times, but she's the only family I have left. I want to be there for her whenever she needs me."

His hand cupped her face, sweetly, familiarly. "I guess you'll be glad when the roads reopen and you can be on your way again."

Three days ago she'd have welcomed the idea, but now.... "Yes," she said weakly, "I can hardly wait."

"It hasn't been much of a Christmas for you so far, has it?"

"It's been...." A change from the usual, unexpected, novel: the trite responses lined up in her mind, waiting to see which one best fit the occasion, because Miss Jessica Simms, headmistress, charted her life by just such conventions. But she hadn't counted on her gaze slipping to his mouth, so near to hers, so incredibly sexy. "Wonderful," she finished on a sigh.

His breath, sweet as mountain air, fanned her face. His fingers, cool against her suddenly fevered skin, traced a line from her cheek to her jaw and slid around her neck. His head obscured the waning sun as he narrowed the last few inches separating her from him. "It has, hasn't it?"

"Yes," she whispered, and closed her eyes as he lavished kisses on her mouth, first at one corner and then the other, and, finally, full on her waiting lips. Beneath his artful persuasion, she opened herself to him and wondered, as his kiss deepened to claim her soul yet again, how she'd ever bring herself to say goodbye to him when the time came for her to leave.

"I think," he murmured huskily, at last dragging his lips from hers, "that we'd better stop while we're ahead. This isn't making-love weather, even with buffalo robes to keep out the cold."

She didn't know why not. She was on fire for him. But should she say so? Could she even begin to scrape up the courage to tell him that, for her, things had changed, that she wasn't the same hidebound woman he'd rescued just a few days before, that she'd fallen in love with a man because of the gentleness that underlay his strength, because of the humor and passion that marked his life in ways they'd never touched hers?

Of course not! Because, at heart, she hadn't changed. That she was hankering for all the traditional trappings of commitment and happy-ever-after romance to validate what they'd both agreed would be a passing affair was proof enough of that. "I agree," she murmured, with admirable restraint. "And we should be getting back to the house. Clancy will be wondering what we're up to."

"I suspect he's figured it out pretty accurately," Morgan said ruefully, sliding back to his side of the seat and stuffing his hands into his gloves before picking up the reins. "But you're right—we should be heading back. I should give him a hand settling the horses for the night and you've got dinner to prepare.''

Why did she allow it to hurt her that, despite the intimacies they'd shared, he was able so easily to assign her to the position of housekeeper again? He'd never promised her a different or more permanent role, after all, and hadn't caring for others and making sure things were done right always been the part that suited her best?

Face it, Jessica, she scolded herself, drawing the hood up over her head again, you've never been the type that men want to die for. Be grateful for the brief happiness you've found here and let it be enough. Don't spoil it by wishing for the impossible.

And yet, despite knowing all that, she heard herself say, ''Why, if this time we've shared has been so wonderful for both of us, does it have to end with my leaving here, Morgan?''

He turned Jasper in a wide circle and waited until they were headed back along the ridge toward the house before he answered. ''Because,'' he said, ''I can't commit beyond this time. What you see here, what you think you know, is only part of the man I am.''

''And the other part?'' she asked, recognizing the absolute truth of what he said. ''What about him?''

He sighed and shook his head. ''That's the part that worries me.''

''You've been honest with me and that's what matters.'' The words burned themselves into his brain the entire time he was putting the cutter away in the unused barn behind the stables.

The problem was not just that he hadn't told her about Parrish; that could easily be remedied. It was the more difficult truth he was having difficulty with, the one which extended to admitting that he was falling in love with her, that he wanted her to remain in his life after these few days were over. And the hardest truth of all

was facing the fact that he had no right to ask that of
her.

"Didn't think I'd be seeing you out here again today," Clancy observed sourly when Morgan led Jasper
back into the stable. "Kinda thought you'd be so plumb
wore out you wouldn't be much use to anyone, seeing
as how you didn't get near enough sleep last night."

"Can it, Clancy. I've got enough on my mind without
you adding your two bits' worth."

"That sweet woman's falling for you, Morgan,"
Clancy persisted, undaunted, "and I want to know what
you plan to do about it."

"What the hell do you expect me to do?" Frustrated,
Morgan stabbed viciously at the nearest bale of straw
with the pitchfork.

"Speakin' the truth wouldn't be a bad place to start."

As if he hadn't already figured out that much! "And
tell her what? That she's welcome to bunk down here
until the weather breaks but that there's a madman out
there somewhere gunning for me and she could end up
being murdered in her bed?"

"T'ain't what Gabriel Parrish might do to her in her
bed that's worryin' me at this precise moment, it's you.
I don't plan to stand by and watch her dismissed as if
she weren't nothing more than a servant around here
when it's plain—"

"I thought you wanted her gone!"

"Of course I did, you dad-blamed fool! I wanted her
as far away as she could get. Far enough that she
wouldn't get splattered with the dirt that follows you
around, but you fooled around too long and left it too
late." He drew an irate breath. "So help me, Morgan
Kincaid, if that woman gets herself hurt at this stage
because you were too damned selfish to keep your drawers done up, I'll—"

"You're out of line, Clancy! Furthermore—"

The sudden shrilling of the telephone hanging on the
wall near the door blasted the rest of his sentence into

oblivion. For a second, he and Clancy glared at each other in frozen silence.

"Well," Clancy finally said, after the third ring, "which one of us is goin' to answer that, Morgan? Or are we just goin' to stand here gapin' at it till the damn thing rings off the wall?"

The ducks were in the oven, stuffed with wild rice and basted with a cranberry glaze. The sparkling white burgundy Morgan had set aside for dinner cooled in a silver ice bucket. The tree glowed in the living room, its light augmented by the flames flickering in the hearth. The table was decked out with the fine family silver and crystal.

Stepping into the shower, Jessica let the hot water pelt over her hair and down her body, welcoming the stinging spray. She had never felt more alive, or more complete.

"I guess I'm wondering where we go from here," he'd said that afternoon, and she'd sensed the same bewildered hunger in him that ate at her. "Yesterday, I thought I knew. Today, I'm not so sure."

Tipping shampoo into the palm of her hand, she scrubbed at her scalp, glad she'd have time enough to dry her hair and leave it lying soft and loose around her face instead of taming it into its usual loop while it was still damp.

Regretfully she thought of the elegant midnight-blue dinner dress she'd worn to the board of governors' Christmas cocktail party and wished she had it with her now. But how could she have known, last week when she'd crammed things into her suitcase before flinging it into the back of her car and setting out on the long drive to Whistling Valley, that she'd be wanting to dress up for a man she'd yet to meet? That was Selena's sort of scenario, not hers.

Would he come to her again tonight? Would they make love again? Was she crazy to believe that perhaps their relationship didn't have to end when she left the ranch?

Tilting her head to one side, she squeezed the excess water from her hair and swathed it in a towel. Already it was dark outside, and another night full of stars and promised moonlight upon them. Christmas night, and the most special she'd ever known.

Humming to herself, she patted her body dry. Powdered and perfumed it, and slipped into the ribboned black satin lingerie with its rich edging of French lace. Rolled cobweb-fine silk stockings up her legs and gave an involuntary shiver of pleasure at the remembered touch of Morgan's hands, the first time he'd touched her bare thigh.

The black silk blouse, the straight black velvet skirt, a cameo that had belonged to her mother and the pearl ear studs without which she was seldom seen, and she was ready, except for putting the finishing touches to her hair.

Over the whine of the hairdryer, she thought she heard the back door slam open, signaling Morgan's return. He'd want to shower, too, before they sat down to dinner. Fluffing the last damp curl into place, she swept a final glance at herself in the full-length mirror and left the room.

Not until she reached the foot of the stairs did she realize that he hadn't come back alone. Clancy was with him, still wearing the same blue denim dungarees he'd worn all day. They stood in the doorway to the living room, waiting for her. Was she going to have to scold them into changing for dinner?

Stepping forward with a smile, she said, "You're back early."

"The roads are open again," Clancy said, an odd reply even without the accompanying grimness of tone.

Her heart stumbled a warning which she ignored. "So?"

"There's nothing to keep you here," he said.

Her heart tripped again, an ominous, unsettling occurrence that left her feeling slightly sick. "Are you…am I being…?"

She left the questions dangling and shook her head at the foolish notion that she was being quite literally kicked out of the house on Christmas night. "Morgan?"

He met her gaze unflinchingly and there was nothing in his eyes—no desire, no passion, no shame. "It's time you were on your way," he said, confirming fears that should have been outlandish but which were, suddenly, all too real. "Get your things and I'll drive you to Sentinel Pass."

"Wait a minute!" she cried. "How do you know the road's open again and what's the sudden rush to be rid of me?"

"We got a phone call, woman," Clancy declared. "And, like Morgan said, it's time you got on the road again before the next storm hits."

"Wouldn't you at least like me to serve dinner first?" she pleaded, and cringed inwardly that she should degrade herself like that. Where was her pride, her self-respect?

"We can serve ourselves," Morgan said bleakly. "Please, Jessica, it's best not to prolong this."

Prolong what? They had been happy together as recently as two hours ago. He had hinted that they might have a future together. What had happened to change things so dramatically?

She looked again from his face to Clancy's and saw the same stubborn determination stamped on the old man's features. "You've done this, haven't you?" she whispered. "You've talked him out of—"

"Clancy has nothing to do with this," Morgan said. "It's a simple matter of making the most of improved conditions while they last. I know how anxious you are to see your sister."

The dismissal was unmistakable, echoing in his voice, reflecting bleakly in his eyes. Had she been deluding herself to think he'd ever shown her a hint of tenderness? Had those unsmiling lips ever softened against hers in a kiss?

"Oh, Lord!" she mumbled, feeling her mouth begin to tremble and seeing Morgan's image blur as her eyes filled with tears. It was the same old story she'd tried to write a hundred times, one in which she insinuated herself into a home, a family. As if baking a few tarts or mopping a floor were enough to earn a place in anyone's heart, least of all a man like Morgan Kincaid who must have women taking a number and lining up to keep him company!

"Bring the truck round to the front while I go get her things, Clancy," she heard him say as she strove to deal with the thudding lurch of her heart as it raced to absorb the blow it had been dealt.

He moved out of her line of vision and left her staring at the teary sparkle of lights on the tree that she'd so lovingly dressed in its best for this special time of year.

She should have chosen the artificial tree with its chi-chi decor, she thought bitterly. It might have reminded her that nothing about this Christmas was permanent or real.

Soon—too soon—he came back down the stairs with her suitcase and bag. He opened the front door and Clancy was there, waiting to relieve him of his load. Turning back, Morgan took her coat, the mohair coat he'd dismissed so cuttingly as being no more appropriate than a party dress at a funeral, and held it out for her.

Numbly, she slid her arms into the sleeves, then stood there like a child while he did up the buttons. When he'd finished, he indicated her west coast city boots that had also earned his scorn. "Put them on," he said, and obediently she stepped into them.

"Good." He blew out a breath of relief. "Let's go."

"No," she said, emerging from the almost hypnotic trance that had taken hold, "Not until you make me understand."

"Not here," he insisted. "We'll have time to talk in the truck."

But the time passed too quickly, he saw to that, taking the road at such reckless speed that, if she'd cared a scrap about living to see another day, she'd have thought he was trying to kill them both.

"We've imposed on your good nature long enough," he dared to say, at one point.

"That's certainly a unique way to describe what we've shared," she replied, growing anger reviving some of her fire.

His profile, illuminated by the dim green glow from the dashboard, gave nothing away. "What would you like me to call it, Jessica?"

"Oh, I don't know." She waved a deliberately languid hand but her voice was edged with pure steel. "A wild, explosive attraction based on nothing but proximity, perhaps? Sexual favors in return for domestic service?"

That elicited a response! He swore, spitting out a socially unacceptable four-letter word that crudely described what she'd have called making love until he'd relieved her of any such illusion.

"Yes," she said, Miss Simms the headmistress resurrecting herself too late to reverse the damage he'd done, "I dare say that's how you would describe it. You must forgive me for not having had the good sense to recognize that sooner."

Enraged, he slammed his gloved hands against the steering wheel. "Goddammit, Jessica, that's not what I'm saying."

"Really? You could have fooled me—did, in fact." The last words wobbled embarrassingly. Biting the inside of her cheek, she steeled herself not to break down in front of him. "But that's all right, Morgan. I've been made a fool of before by better men than you."

"Stuart, you mean?" He ground out the question with

barely restrained fury. "Hell, Jessica, I don't deserve that."

Ahead, a sprinkling of lights showed in the dark. Subduing the urge to let him know exactly what she thought he did deserve, she said coolly, "Are we almost there?"

"Yes." He swung around a curve that ran parallel to a frozen river winding along the valley floor. "We'll be at Stedman's service station in about five minutes."

Time had never flown so fast. The seconds slipped away from her like her life's blood and there was nothing she could think of to halt their progress, nothing she could say to change his mind. All she could do was try to find an answer. "Why did you ever let me into your life, Morgan?"

"Because when I first started...working, a man murdered a young woman while she was on her way home from seeing a movie with her girlfriend," he said as the first buildings appeared. "She'd walked the last few blocks alone and was killed almost within sight of the house she lived in when it happened."

Ignoring Jessica's murmur of sympathy, he continued, "She was nineteen, the same age as my sister at the time, and the tragedy of it struck home to me in a way I'll never forget. I vowed then that I'd never knowingly let the same thing happen to another woman if I could possibly prevent it."

"So you rescued me for my own good," Jessica said bitterly. "Was that why you made love to me, too?"

He sighed heavily. "No, Jessica. But I thought I knew myself well enough not to contemplate the idea of re-marrying. I've never had reason to re-evaluate that decision until the last few days."

Was she supposed to feel better, knowing he'd had to think twice before rejecting her? Don't hand me placebos, she wanted to shriek. I don't want to be your almost-ran!

"I quite understand," she said stonily. "I, too, decided commitment to one individual is a poor investment and made my work my life. And although I am fond of my students I always hold something back.'' She paused, struggling to contain the pain that howled within her, then uttered the last lie she'd ever tell him. ''I never give *everything* to anyone, any more.''

The flashing lights in the window of the service station flung red and yellow ribbons out into the road. Steering between the high-banked snow left by the plows, Morgan swung into the parking lot and brought the truck to a halt.

Leaving the engine idling, he turned in his seat to face her. ''I guess we both made the right decision, then.''

She looked at him feature by feature, committing him to memory and wondering how long it would be before the image blurred enough around the edges for her to forget how blue his eyes were, how thick and dark his lashes, how sexy his mouth. How many nights would she awake from dreaming of him and find herself weeping for the loss?

''I guess we did,'' she said.

He swung open his driver's-side door. ''I'll give you a hand with your suitcase.''

''No,'' she said. ''Don't bother. We'll just say goodbye here and get it over with.''

''You're right.'' He pulled off his glove.

Oh, please! she thought. Don't ask me to shake hands and part friends!

He touched her face. He leaned forward. ''Goodbye, Jessica,'' he said huskily, and kissed her lightly not quite on the mouth.

CHAPTER TEN

JESSICA stood in the bitterly cold parking lot, watching Morgan drive away. As his brake lights disappeared around the bend, a spasm of grief clutched her, for the love she had briefly known, for the beauty he had brought into her life.

Swallowing to relieve the ache in her throat, she gave herself a mental shake. Enough! It was over. The real world waited—her world of dependable older sister, of conscientious headmistress. Sober, practical roles for which she was so eminently well suited.

Picking up her bags, she turned toward the service station. Inside, the air was thick and stale with tobacco smoke. On the counter next to the cash register stood a tiny lopsided tree, its spindly branches looped with a dusty foil garland. On the wall behind hung an assortment of flashlight batteries, fishing lures, windshield scrapers and other sundry items. Tire chains and sacks of road salt were stacked to one side on the floor.

A horseshoe-shaped lunch counter filled the other half of the room. Three hefty men, truckers probably, judging by the semis she'd noticed parked outside, straddled stools closest to a serving hatch and joked with the middle-aged waitress busy wiping the tops of plastic ketchup bottles with a damp rag. At the other end, a slender man hunched over a bowl of soup.

From a television set mounted on the wall, a well-known singer hosted her annual Christmas show amid a glitter of sequins and special effects. The orchestra played "Let It Snow".

The truckers spared Jessica a cursory glance. The lone

man ignored her, his attention split between his soup and the TV show.

"Ma'am?" A young mechanic in blue overalls appeared from a side door. "You looking for a fill-up of gas?"

"I'm looking for my car," Jessica told him. "It was towed in three days ago for repairs and I believe it's ready for me now."

"Heck, yes, the maroon Taurus. Mr. Kincaid's man phoned not half an hour ago to make sure it would be ready for you when you got here. We're still working on it, but it shouldn't be too much longer." He wiped greasy hands on a rag and shrugged apologetically. "Things are a bit backed up with all the weather we've been getting. Have a seat while you're waiting, why don't you?"

She nodded, too dispirited to argue. Morgan's anxiety to be rid of her, even though it meant her waiting around in this godforsaken outpost of civilization, added fresh insult to injury.

"Hey, Linda!" the young man yelled to the waitress. "Get the lady here a cup of coffee." He glanced again at Jessica. "You hungry, ma'am? Marty, the cook, makes a mean hot turkey sandwich."

The mere thought sent her stomach into revolt. "No, thanks. Just coffee will be fine."

Climbing onto a stool equidistant from the other customers, she propped her elbow on the counter and rested her chin on her hand.

"You goin' far, miss?" Linda, the waitress, plunked a thick mug down in front of her and filled it with coffee from the Thermos jug.

"Whistling Valley ski resort."

Linda pursed disapproving lips. "Rotten night to be driving. You take care, you hear? You'd've been better off to wait up at Mr. Kincaid's place till conditions improved. Road's only been open a couple of hours and littered with more abandoned cars than a scrap yard."

She jerked her head toward the truckers. "The boys here say tryin' to get past them all is worse than running a slalom course down a foggy mountain."

"Maybe I'll check into a motel." Jessica poured cream into her coffee.

"Ain't no motel before Wintercreek and that's another eighty miles down the highway. You get that far, you might as well go the rest of the way and be done with it." The waitress hitched her bosom onto the counter and leaned forward confidentially. "You sure you wouldn't rather go back to the Kincaid ranch? Morgan ain't the type to turn a person away on Christmas night, 'specially not a woman traveling on her own."

"My sister's been hospitalized in Whistling Valley and I'm anxious to see her."

"Better to wait till it's light out, just the same. Ain't no point in both of you ending up in hospital."

"Mr. Kincaid didn't seem to think I'd have any trouble getting through," Jessica said, wondering why she was even bothering to argue the point. "In any case, I'm not sure I could find my way back to the ranch in the dark."

"Ain't no problem, honey." The waitress licked the point of a stubby pencil, tore a sheet from her order pad and proceeded to draw a map. "You're here, see? You just follow the road east till you come to the bridge, then, about a hundred yards past, there's a bit of a rise...."

She droned on good-naturedly. Too weary and heartsick to stop her, Jessica feigned interest and prayed for deliverance. Drumming up a smile of thanks when the discourse finally ended, she placed the completed map next to her coffee cup and heaved a quiet sigh of relief when the waitress turned her attention to serving the truckers slabs of apple pie.

"I'm headed west on the highway and can show you the way, if you like."

Startled, Jessica swiveled on her stool and realized the

man from the far end of the counter had moved and was now standing close behind her.

His jacket collar was drawn up close around his neck and he wore a black wool hat pulled so far down that it almost touched the rims of his heavily tinted glasses. He was well-spoken and looked harmless enough—at least, from what she could see of him—but she'd had enough of accepting kindness from strangers. "Thank you, but I really do have to get to Whistling Valley."

"Suit yourself." He shrugged, a tight smile thinning his narrow lips, and moved away again.

Just then the mechanic reappeared and came to perch on the stool next to Jessica's. "All set, ma'am. Car'll be brought around the front in about five minutes and filled up so you can be on your way."

"Thank you." Relieved, she finished her coffee. "How much do I owe?"

"Not a thing. Coffee's on the house and Mr. Kincaid's taken care of everything else."

Not quite everything, she thought. You couldn't put a price on a crushed heart.

"Hey, Linda!" One of the truckers banged a meaty fist on the counter. "Switch the TV to the news channel, will ya, and let's see what the weatherman's promising for tomorrow? Wouldn't mind getting home before the kids forget what I gave them for Christmas."

"I just need a signature here, ma'am." The mechanic pushed forward a work order and indicated the place. "To say you got your vehicle back with the repairs done to your satisfaction, you understand?"

Jessica scribbled her name, aware of a blast of icy air snaking around her ankles as the outside door opened behind her.

"Might as well stay put where it's warm, honey," the waitress advised, seeing Jessica preparing to leave. "Five minutes, Charlie said, and there ain't no sense hangin' around outside freezin' your butt off all that time." She hefted the coffee Thermos across the counter. "Have another on the house while you wait."

Sweet heaven, Jessica thought wearily, was she never going to sever the ties binding her to Morgan Kincaid's world?

"...conditions expected to hold another day, allowing Christmas travelers delayed by the weather to finally reach their destinations."

Half-heartedly, Jessica turned her attention to the TV newsman, sprig of holly in his lapel, his jovial tone deepening to assume a more somber note as he continued, "On a different front, escaped prison inmate Gabriel Parrish, believed to be headed west in what police are calling a personal vendetta against the man who put him behind bars for the murder of twenty-one-year-old Sally Blackman almost ten years ago, was reportedly seen in the Rosemont area."

The picture on the screen changed to reveal a head shot of the fugitive. Short, greying hair, deep-set, intense dark eyes, and something about the cast of the pinched, unsmiling mouth that struck a strangely familiar chord. Where had she seen it before?

Frowning, she turned her attention to the newscast again.

"...leaving behind a clear trail of evidence. A family planning to spend the holidays in their ski cabin arrived to discover the place broken into and several items missing, including men's clothing, a hand gun, and a small amount of cash," the announcer said. "Their neighbor also reported a stolen snowmobile, since recovered close to Sentinel Pass, a truck stop not far from where crown prosecutor Morgan Kincaid, the man who brought Parrish to justice, owns recreational property. Parrish is considered armed and dangerous—"

Morgan Kincaid, crown prosecutor...the man who brought a convicted killer to justice? Why had he let her believe he was a simple rancher? And what other lies had he told her?

"Car's all ready to roll, Miss Simms." Charlie, the mechanic, swung open the outside door, poked his head inside and waved cheerfully.

A stolen snowmobile, since recovered close to Sentinel Pass, a truck stop.... Halfway to the door Jessica stopped, a thrill of horror trembling over her.

She cast a frantic glance around the room. The truckers continued to watch the screen. Linda emptied dirty ashtrays into a container. And the man with the tinted glasses and low-slung hat—the man with the disturbingly narrow, pinched mouth?

He had disappeared silently into the night. And so had the rough map showing the Kincaid ranch, which Jessica had left next to her coffee mug.

Except for a solitary light burning in Clancy's quarters, they'd left the house and stables in darkness. That way, it was easier to see anyone approaching the house.

The weather continued to cooperate, flooding the countryside with moonlight. Morgan sat at his bedroom window, unwillingly recalling the night before. Her laughter as he'd pulled her onto the ice, the slenderness of her as they'd danced, the naked desire that had clawed at him until he'd found surcease in her embrace....

He blinked fiercely, willing the images, the ache, to disappear. He was too savvy by far to have been blindsided by love, surely? And yet how else did he define the emotions tearing at him now, when all his energy and attention should be directed on the showdown fast approaching?

"Tell me again what they said when they phoned, Morgan." From his post on the other side of the window, Clancy flexed his arthritic leg.

"That they'd got through to us as soon as the lines were repaired."

"I know that, you damn fool! What else?"

"That they'd found a folder in his cell, collating information from every publication you care to name that ever ran a news item on me or my doings. Photographs, gossip, fact, fiction—you name it, he'd hoarded it.''

"Any mention of the ranch?"

"Nothing specific as to its exact location, but enough clues for a man as smart as Parrish to latch onto."

"You sure he'll come lookin' for you here, Morgan?"

"Sure?" Morgan sighed. "As sure as gut instinct and circumstantial evidence can be. He's headed this way, Clancy. I can feel it in my bones."

"You did the right thing, then, getting Jessica out of here as quick as you did."

The ache intensified, spearing him straight through the heart at the memory of her standing alone in the Stedman's parking lot, dumped yet again by someone she'd thought she could trust. "Pity it's the only right thing I did where she was concerned."

They lapsed into silence again, each buried in his own thoughts. The minutes ticked by heavily, a time bomb playing a waiting game.

"It doesn't have to be this way," Clancy said, never taking his eyes from the slim curve of the road as it disappeared beyond the windbreak. "You could call in the law."

"I am the law," Morgan said.

"Reinforcements, then." Clancy stroked the oiled stock of the rifle slung across his knees.

"No. He's out there, watching, waiting. He'd just stay hidden till they were gone. I might as well settle this once and for all."

"Never figured you for a man with a death wish, Morgan."

"I don't plan to die."

"Got something special to live for, have you?"

Morgan felt Clancy's gaze slew sideways and bore into him. "Haven't you?" he said evenly.

"Nothing like Jessica Simms. Reckon you've—"

"He's coming." Morgan's whisper cut into the night as cleanly as a knife blade. "I saw the flash of lights from a car or something as it came around the last bend beyond the pines.''

Clancy leaned forward, his gaze raking the inky shadow of trees on snow. "You sure? Don't seem likely he'd announce his arrival like that, Morgan.''

"I'm sure.'' Silently, Morgan stepped to the corner of the room and lifted the shotgun from its resting place by the wall. "He's here, Clancy.''

"Son of a gun!'' Clancy exhaled sharply. "Someone's here all right, driving right up to the front door bold as brass, so it can't be Parrish.''

Swinging back to the window, Morgan cursed as a familiar maroon sedan slid to a stop at the foot of the steps. "That's Jessica's car.''

"God Almighty,'' Clancy whispered in horror. "You're right, Morgan. And she ain't come alone.''

She brought the car to a halt at the foot of the steps. It had been easy to find the house, once she'd made the turn from the main highway. Morgan's tire tracks were plain to see in the bright white moonlight and all she'd had to do was follow them.

"That's right, dear.'' The pleasant, cultured voice filled her with terror. "Slide out of the car slowly and remember I'm right behind you. Morgan will be so surprised to see us, don't you think?''

He was mad. She had realized it from the moment his voice had floated from the back seat, just as she'd headed back along the highway to warn Morgan and Clancy. "How kind of you, my dear,'' he'd crooned, "to chauffeur me the last few miles of my long journey.''

As if the realization that she had an escaped felon for a passenger hadn't been fright enough, he'd kept the cold tip of a gun pressed to the back of her neck throughout the journey and spent the entire time it had taken her to drive the distance to the Kincaid ranch spewing out in silky tones his venom for Morgan, and for her.

"Slut," he'd said, as pleasantly as any other person might have said "Have a lovely day". "You slept with him, didn't you? I could see it in your eyes, back there in that disgusting greasy spoon of a diner where we met, when that pathetic fool of a waitress mentioned his name. You had that look about you, of a woman scorned."

Now, as she stepped out of the car, she searched for a way to distract him just long enough to escape into the house. "What are you going to do next?" she asked, clinging to the door frame as her feet slithered on the packed snow.

"Why, we're going to pay a little visit to your lover," he said, his breath drifting revoltingly over her face as he sidled up next to her and took her other arm. "Oh, look, he's come to welcome us! Isn't that sociable of him?"

A sudden blaze of light accompanied his words. Morgan stood silhouetted in the open front door of the house, a large gun held loosely in his hands. "Let her go, Parrish," he said coldly. "You've got no quarrel with her."

"Put the shotgun away, dear boy," Parrish cooed, jabbing the nasty little revolver to her temple, "or I'll be obliged to shoot your little whore."

Carefully, Morgan laid his firearm on the floor of the veranda and started slowly down the steps.

"Stay away," Parrish warned, his voice rising dangerously. "Come any closer and she'll die, Kincaid, just like the other one did."

"You don't want to kill her," Morgan replied calmly, continuing his descent. "You'll never be a free man again, if you do."

"I'm already free," Parrish said, raising his arm and pointing the revolver straight at Morgan's chest.

"Not for long," Morgan assured him, reaching the last step.

"For as long as it takes," the madman squealed, his

grip on Jessica's arm slackening as his voice ran manically out of control.

It was at best a slender chance, but it was the only one to present itself. Desperately, she flung herself forward, catching him off guard and swinging the front door of her car toward him with all her strength. He saw it coming and let her go as he tried to fend it off and at the same time retain his footing on the treacherous ice.

Simultaneously, Morgan leaped the remaining distance between them, landing half on top of Jessica, with enough impact to knock the breath out of her, and half on top of Parrish.

She was aware of a scuffle, of grunts of pain. Of bodies rolling in the snow and the glint of cold metal in moonlight as Parrish swung his revolver in the air. She saw Morgan lunging after it, saw Parrish's insane grin as he aimed straight for Morgan's head.

She heard the sickening impact of a bullet hitting flesh, and her own scream of agonized fear as both men slumped to the frozen ground.

"Morgan!" she wept, crawling forward on her hands and knees, beside herself at the pool of blood staining the snow where he lay beneath Parrish.

"Stay where you are, woman, till I'm sure I've disabled the critter."

The words came to her from a distance, fogged by an overwhelming sense of misery unequalled by anything she'd experienced at Stuart or her aunt's hands.

Slowly she looked up to discover Clancy's familiar scowl hovering above her, and thought it was the second most beautiful sight she'd ever seen. The first was Morgan, heaving Parrish aside and retrieving the revolver which had slid half under her car.

"Wonder where he got this little beauty?" he remarked, as casually as though he played Russian roulette with his life every other day of the week.

"What does it matter?" she shrieked, reaction setting in and sending the tears streaming down her face. "That lunatic almost killed you! For pity's sake, Morgan, he almost killed both of us! Why didn't you tell me what's been going on? Or didn't it strike you as being any of my business?''

"I did my level best not to make it your business, Jessica." He poked at Parrish with his foot, at which the injured man let out a howl of pain. "You got him right in the shoulder, Clancy. Just enough to put him out of action till I get him locked up again."

"Intended to," Clancy said with pride. "Not that I had much choice, seeing as how you were about to get yourself blown to kingdom come. Hell, boy, if I can shoot a rat's ass at a hundred yards, I can nail scum like Parrish *exactly* where it'll do the most good. Don't reckon he'll be giving anyone too much grief for the next little while."

"You got through to the police?"

"RCMP are on their way. Stop your sniveling long enough, woman, and you'll hear the sirens," he added severely to Jessica, who leaned against the hood of her car, openly sobbing.

"What the hell," Morgan said softly, pulling her into the shelter of his arms. "You're in shock, sweetheart. Let's get you inside and away from this mess."

He led her up the steps and into the living room and seated her tenderly on the couch. Dazed, she stared around her, at the unlit Christmas tree, at the dying embers in the hearth, at the table she'd set for three...how long ago?

Morgan brought her a glass half-filled with brandy. "Here," he said. "Drink this."

She looked up through a sparkle of tears—at the shimmering crystal in his hand, at his long, lean body that had come so close to being torn apart by violence.

What if she hadn't heard the news report? What if she'd gone on her way, full of bitterness and wishing that the misery he'd doled out to her would come back to haunt him threefold, then found out when it was too late that the man she'd fallen in love with had sent her away so that he could play hero in a drama guaranteed to have no happy ending? What if he'd been killed and left her to cope with the guilt of knowing she'd come close to hating him for the way he'd hustled her out of his home and his life?

How dared he? The tears rolled down her face afresh, hot streams of them, fueled by anger. "How could you do this to me?" she sobbed, dashing the glass from his hand. "How could you have lied to me, over and over again?"

He slumped beside her on the couch. "To protect you," he said bleakly.

"Protect me from what? From falling in love with you?" Her voice rose in anguish. "Is *that* why you slept with me, Morgan? To protect me? Well, excuse me for not appreciating the gesture!"

"Honey," he said, trying to draw her into his arms. "Sweetheart—"

"Don't touch me!" She scooted to the far end of the couch, her body racked by violent shivers. "I was just a diversion, something to keep you amused until the real action began, wasn't I?"

"No," he protested, refusing to keep his distance. "Jessica, honey, if I'd realized when I met you what sort of trouble was waiting, I'd never have brought you here. By the time I knew the score, it was too late— there was no place else I could send you. I thought, as long as the roads were impassable, you'd be as safe here as anywhere."

He lifted his hands to touch her, then let them drop helplessly when she flinched away from him. "I knew that Parrish couldn't get very far as long as the snow kept up, and that the police would be looking for him, but I never expected that we'd...that you and I would—"

"What?" she spat. "Climb between the sheets? Roll in the hay? *Screw?*"

Sweet heaven, where had socially correct, morally up-right Miss Simms gone, and who was this shrew scream-ing obscenities at the man who'd just saved her life?

"It wasn't like that, Jessica," he said, "and I'm sorry if I handled myself in such a way that that's the im-pression I gave you. I know all about society's misfits and the ills they confer. I'm expert at unraveling other people's truths from the web of deceit behind which they camouflage them, but I guess I don't know squat about showing a woman I love her."

"No, you don't," she sobbed, stoking her anger with a fury born of heartache and delayed fear. "I should have let that madman blow your brains out...."

"Yes, sweetheart," Morgan said soothingly, circling his arms around her despite her best efforts to elude him.

"Except he'd never have been able to find them...."

"No, darling. Hush now and let me hold you."

"Police have arrived and want to talk to you, Mor-gan," Clancy said from the doorway. "Shall I bring 'em in here?"

"No," Morgan said, releasing her and standing up. "I'll see them in the office."

The chill left behind where his arms had been cut her to the bone. "Woman," Clancy declared wrathfully, throwing a handful of kindling into the fireplace and stirring the embers to life, "we could all use a fresh pot of coffee. And if you really want to make yourself useful you could make more tarts."

"I am not your kitchen lackey," she retorted, um-brage reviving something of her usual starch.

He grinned at her over his shoulder. "But you're Mor-gan's woman, ain't you?"

"No," she said. "I most certainly am not."

He grinned for the second time in a minute, an un-heard-of occurrence in Jessica's limited experience. "Try tellin' him that," he advised.

She was a fool to let his words warm her the way she did, an even bigger fool to let her hopes rise from the ashes of her earlier despair. But then, she'd suspected as much, practically from the moment she'd first set eyes on Morgan Kincaid.

"I'll make coffee," she finally agreed, "but you can forget the tarts."

"What the hey?" Clancy snickered. "At least it's a start."

It was the better part of two hours before the police completed their business and Gabriel Parrish had been shipped by ambulance to recover from his wounds in the nearest maximum security penitentiary.

Not long after that, Clancy pulled his usual disappearing act, leering evilly over his shoulder as he left.

"It's his way of saying he approves of our being a couple," Morgan said wryly. "He's quite the romantic under that crusty exterior."

"What Clancy does or doesn't approve of is immaterial," Jessica said sadly. "We are not a couple, Morgan. Couples don't offer protection as an excuse for deceit, they trust each other to cope with the truth."

Spreading his arms wide, leaning both hands on the mantelpiece, he stared at the fire. "And what if the truth divides them, Jessica? Then what?"

"Then they were doomed from the outset. Lies don't strengthen a relationship, Morgan, no matter how well intentioned they might be. They undermine it and eventually they destroy it."

His shoulders sagged at that and it took all the resolve she could muster not to go to him and wrap her arms around him and tell him that none of it mattered as long as they were together.

She hated the fact that her body and heart held such sway and tried to pretend differently, but the awareness, the sheer physical longing, never let up. It growled and paced within her, gnawing away at her defenses no matter how diligently she tried to subdue it.

"I lied to you," he said eventually, his voice weighted

with regret, "for your own good. To keep you safe, to leave you free of fear."

"The blow you dealt me in doing so far exceeds anything Parrish could have done to hurt me," she replied.

He spun around, his face blazing with sudden anger. "You say that now but if I'd told you I was falling in love with you and wanted a future with you how long would it have been before you'd decided I wasn't worth the risk?"

"Never," she said. "Because love involves risk. It means trust and acceptance and passion all bound together by truth. No games, no artifice, no promises that can't be kept, just the pledge that tomorrow or next week or fifty years from now the feelings will still be there—stronger, surer, no matter what."

"There was a time, when I was first married, when I'd have agreed with you but the rot set in anyway, so subtly that I never knew for sure just when it started."

"There must have been signs, Morgan. Marriages don't fall apart overnight."

"Oh, there were signs, all right. My work became the other woman, at least in my ex-wife's eyes. She resented my involvement with what she called 'the seamy underside of the law'. Suddenly, what she'd once perceived as respectable and even honorable became a lifestyle liability, a threat to her peace of mind. And who's to say she wasn't right?"

An explosive sigh burst from him, seeming to tear its way free. "You say you want the truth, Jessica? Well, here's the truth of my life when I'm not kicking back up here and breathing the clean country air: I put criminals away. If I'm ever appointed to the Bench—and there are rumors I might be—they'd probably call me the hanging judge because *I do not believe anyone should break the law with impunity*."

"You're shouting at me and there's no need," Jessica said. "I happen to agree with you. You don't have to convince me."

"But what if you were married to me? Could you handle the occasional hate mail, the vicious, anonymous phone calls that would find our home no matter how often we changed to another unlisted number? Could you survive hearing the insults hurled at your husband by a man facing a prison term? Because Daphne couldn't. 'No woman should have to live with this kind of harassment,' she told me, when she finally bowed out of the marriage.''

"Didn't you try to talk her out of it?"

"No," he said. "By then I no longer cared enough to try. So don't tell me that love means acceptance or the pledge that it will survive, no matter what, because I'm here to tell you it doesn't always work out like that."

Jessica felt a profound sadness then, for him, for them. He might profess to be falling in love with her but how did they stand a chance of finding happiness if, from the outset, he expected they'd fail? He seemed so strong, so confident, and yet he was as lonely and isolated in his way as she was in hers. When had he stopped believing he deserved some satisfaction for a job well done?

"Doesn't anyone ever take the time to tell you you make a difference?" she asked him. "Or that the world is a better place for having men like you in it?"

"Oh, I have my fans," he said wryly, "but the people I'm most likely to hear from are those who feel I've ruined their lives. Gabriel Parrish is a case in point and I wish I could tell you he's the last, but I can't. The world is full of wing nuts, sweetheart, and the best I can promise any woman is that I'll stand between her and danger whenever I see it headed our way, but that's hardly a guarantee likely to inspire her to making a lifetime commitment to me."

Could she, if he were to ask her? Jessica looked down at her hands, knotted together in her lap, evidence that the trauma of the last few hours still lingered.

She hadn't coped very well tonight. She didn't think she'd ever cope well with that kind of situation. What if he was right and the odds were against her? Did either of them need the burden of another failed relationship?

"Tell me what you're thinking," he said, when the silence grew too oppressive.

She gave a little shrug and sighed. "I think we're making a mistake even discussing the possibility of such a commitment when we've known each other so short a time and clearly have much more to learn."

He smiled. "Well, you're a lot more sensible than Daphne ever was; that I have to admit."

Sensible. The word had dogged her from childhood and she hated it. But it was hard to shake off its influence after so many years and follow a different course.

She wanted to go to him, to have him sweep her up in his strong arms and carry her up to his room. She wanted him to strip away her clothes and cover her with kisses. She wanted him to unleash her sexuality again and make her forget every other consideration but that they needed each other in a way that defied sensible or proper or logical.

She took a deep breath and screwed up her courage to tell him so. But how? What were the right words? *Where* were they? "May I stay here tonight?" she said, praying he'd hear what she was really asking.

He searched her face, then looked away to the moon-streaked darkness beyond the window. "Yes," he said. "Of course. Your room's still here and it's much too late for you to think of driving any further tonight after all that's happened. You'll face the journey much better in the morning when you've had some rest."

"I suppose." Still, she lingered, longing for him to argue her point, to convince her that time didn't count when two people shared something as rare and beautiful as they'd found.

But he didn't. Instead he looked at her with a wealth of sadness in his eyes, as though he could read exactly what lay in her heart.

"You have a life, Jessica," he said. "A nice, ordered

life, with everything laid out and run according to rule. I don't. I never know what tomorrow will bring and, to be honest, I'm not sure I want to. I'd like to tell you I can change, that I'm ready for something less hair-raising than what happened here tonight, but I'm not sure I can do that, either.

"I'm falling in love with you. I'd like to think we have a future together. But I have no right to try to sell you a bill of goods until I know for sure exactly what it contains, so please don't ask me to do that. You deserve better. You've been cheated enough.''

CHAPTER ELEVEN

WINTER dragged its heels into a late spring and Jessica went through the motions of running her school. But the routine that had sustained her for so many years had lost its power to heal. She was the custodian only of her students; they were not really hers to love, and even if they had been they would not have eased the ache in her heart.

Only Morgan, whose memory refused to fade, could have accomplished that and he, apparently, had no urge to do so. He had let her walk out of his house and out of his life and made no attempt to stop her.

Selena had been scandalized when she'd heard. It had been her considered opinion that only a complete nincompoop would allow such a "stud muffin" to escape, and that the only thing left to do was go back and fight for him.

Jessica hadn't thought herself capable of finding anything amusing just then, but hearing Morgan described as a stud muffin had elicited a smile. However, she'd refused to follow her sister's advice, determined that, as long as Morgan was the one with all the doubts, he must also be the one to resolve them.

She would not go begging for love again. Actions spoke louder than words and he was the one who'd talked about their finding a future together. If he was serious, he must come to her.

But the days had become weeks and now it was April, with the magnolias in the academic quadrangle in early bloom, and not once in all that time had there been a word from Morgan.

She stared out of her office window, watching as the

last few students left by family car for the Easter break, and could have wept all over again for what she had let slip through her fingers.

It seemed that frivolous Selena, who'd barely managed to scrape through high school, won more prizes where men were concerned than her supposedly clever sister could ever hope to acquire. Pride, Jessica had come to appreciate, was a poor substitute for love.

Squaring her shoulders, she turned to the paperwork waiting for her on her desk. But scholarship grants and budget restraints held no fascination for a mind morbidly curious to know if another woman had leaped at the chance to fill the spot she'd so foolishly vacated.

Was it worth the risk of further heartache to find out?

Yes, she decided. Anything was better than living in a vacuum of uncertainty. Of waiting for the phone to ring, for the mailman to deliver a letter, for a sign, however small, that Morgan had not found he could live very well without her. There had to be closure, one way or the other.

She glanced at the clock above the fireplace and reached a decision. If she put her mind to it, she could finish up what had to be done here and still make the five-thirty ferry sailing to the mainland.

There was no putting things off any longer. Real love didn't conveniently go away. It refused to die, no matter how firmly one ignored it. That much she'd learned over the last three and a half months and if Morgan hadn't, it was time she taught him.

The daily grind of upholding justice regardless of personal cost went on, but the spark, the drive, the caring commitment had grown dim. For years Morgan had successfully looked outside himself to find fulfillment but now, when he needed it the most, satisfaction eluded him. Without her he felt only half alive.

"For a guy who's a shoo-in for promotion, you're

looking pretty grim these days,'' one of his colleagues observed, the week before Easter.

He wasn't the only one to notice the change. ''What's curdlin' your cream?'' Clancy inquired, when Morgan phoned to say he'd changed his mind about spending the long weekend at the ranch. ''Time was you couldn't wait to drag your sorry hide up here.''

''I have other plans,'' Morgan said, arriving at a decision he should have reached weeks ago.

He cleared his appointments by eleven the next morning and arrived at the ferry terminal shortly before noon. It was a fine day with light winds and too few clouds to obscure the sun.

As the stretch of water between the boat and the mainland grew wider and the low-rising hills of the islands took on more distinct shape, he paced an isolated section of the ferry's upper deck, rehearsing what he'd say to her.

He still wasn't sure he'd got it right, even when the announcement came over the loudspeaker that the ferry was approaching Springhill Island and those passengers disembarking there should return to their vehicles.

He was a man used to being in charge, a man who acted and got things done. The nervousness gripping him now was so foreign to him that he hadn't the foggiest clue how to go about dealing with it.

Impatiently he waited for the long line of cars ahead of him to move out of the cavernous hull of the boat. At length he was waved forward and emerged into the sunshine again.

Even as his deck was being cleared, a lower deck was already loading vehicles leaving the island. Just as he left the ramp and pulled onto the road a sleek blue bus with the words ''Springhill Island Private School'' scrolled on its side inched its way down toward the belly of the boat.

Ahead of him a traffic light turned red. Slowing to a stop, he took down the sunglasses clipped to the visor above the windshield and studied the map on the seat beside him. The school lay about thirty miles away, at the southern tip of the island.

He settled back for the drive, the blood which had moved so sluggishly through his veins in the last weeks pumping with tense anticipation. He passed farms, golf courses, yacht basins, old inns and gracious country houses. Offshore, the neighboring islands snoozed in the afternoon sun.

At any other time, he would have found the spectacle delightful. Today, he was too preoccupied trying to control the nervous tension, the like of which not even the most hardened criminal had ever managed to promote in him.

Suddenly, the split rail fence of a dairy farm to the left gave way to a high stone wall and at last—too soon—he was there, passing between iron gates bearing the same gothic scroll as the bus, and following a curving drive lined with flowering dogwoods.

Occasionally, beyond the trees, he caught glimpses of a lake, playing fields, several small houses, and finally came upon the school itself, a dignified ivy-covered Victorian building.

The domed foyer was empty but he could hear women's voices coming from the door marked "GENERAL OFFICE" and also from several of the classrooms surrounding a central courtyard. Feeling oddly out of his element, he approached the office door.

It swung open before he could knock. "Oh!" the pretty young woman facing him exclaimed. "Sorry, I didn't mean to run you down."

"That's okay," he said, and had to clear his throat before he could continue. "I—er—I'd like to speak to...."

He stumbled to a halt, too far removed from his own milieu to feel comfortable, too out of sync with the stomach-churning state of nerves in which he found himself to project his usual air of authority.

This was Jessica's turf. Here, she wasn't the woman who'd filled his life and his bed too briefly but who'd stolen his heart for ever. She was the boss, the one in charge. She could—and might—have him thrown out.

"Yes?" The woman with the books was staring at him, clearly wondering if she had some sort of lunatic on her hands.

Jeez, Kincaid! Get it together!

"I'd like to see the headmistress."

"I didn't know she had another appointment today. Is she expecting you?"

"No," he said apologetically, and wondered how in hell a man of his years and experience could suddenly regress to the maturity level of a boy hauled up on the carpet for breaking the rules. "No, I'm afraid she isn't."

The woman smiled kindly, the way a nurse might before handing over a patient to a sadistic dentist. "Hang on, and I'll see if she's still here. She did say something about catching the last ferry to the mainland."

"When does that sail?" Morgan asked, deciding that if he and Jessica had passed in the lineup of cars at the terminal the gods were definitely having a good laugh at his expense.

"Five-thirty." She dumped an armful of books on a nearby chair and poked her head inside the office again. "Has Jessica left yet?"

"No," an unseen voice replied. "She's in her office as far as I know."

"You're in luck." The pretty woman turned back to him and smiled again. "I'll warn her she's got a visitor. I'm Deirdre Bayliss, grade ten home room teacher and head of the math department, by the way. Whose father are you?"

"I'm not," he said.

Ms. Bayliss's eyes narrowed slightly and her smile wasn't quite as warm when she asked, "Then who shall I say is calling?"

To his disgust Morgan realized his palms were sweating and his shirt collar choking him. "Um...I'd like to surprise her. Pleasantly," he added hastily, at the suspicious glance this aroused. "I'm her...friend. She spent Christmas at my place."

She'd probably kill him for making that little tidbit of news public knowledge, but he'd geared himself up to come here and confront her, was putting himself through hell now he'd arrived, and he wasn't about to be thwarted at this late stage by being refused permission to see her.

"Well, I'm not sure...."

"I know. In this day and age, you can never be too careful." Reaching into his wallet, he withdrew a business card and offered it for her inspection, along with his most winning smile. "I'm harmless, as you can see, but you're welcome to stick around and see for yourself if it'll make you feel better."

He knew Jessica well enough to realize she'd walk barefoot over hot coals before she'd air her private life in front of any member of her staff. If he could just get a foot in her door, she'd allow him to stay and say his piece, no matter how much she might want to kick him out on his rear.

"Well," pretty Deirdre Bayliss allowed, visibly impressed to find herself talking to the senior crown prosecutor of the lower mainland, "I'll see you to the door at least. Follow me."

The budget proposals were read, the mid-term reports signed and her desk was clear. Apart from a couple of minor items she was finished, and should make it to the ferry terminal in plenty of time.

She was at her filing cabinet, with her back to the door, when it opened. "A gentleman to see you, Ms. Simms," Deirdre Bayliss announced, her use of Jessica's surname indicating that the visitor was not someone either expected or known.

Probably another well-heeled parent wanting to see

his daughter pushed to the head of the admissions waiting list, Jessica decided resignedly, sneaking a glance at her watch. He'd pretend otherwise, of course, dangling the offer to underwrite a scholarship or contribute vast sums to the construction of a new wing, but there'd been too many such bribes in the past, usually occurring with a new term about to begin, for her to expect anything different this time.

Well, she'd give him exactly five minutes before she showed him the door. Expression neutral, blood pressure normal, emotions under control, she turned to greet the visitor.

He filled the doorway to the extent that Deirdre had to stand on tiptoe and peer over his shoulder to catch Jessica's eye. And suddenly, after months of hoping and wanting and, finally, of despairing, she was face to face with Morgan again.

Astonishment left her swaying on her feet. She felt the blood drain from her face, bleaching her features with shock. This wasn't happening the way she'd planned! She needed time to prepare herself, to decide how best to approach him.

"Would you like me to stay, Ms. Simms?" Deirdre said, alarm threading her voice.

She feared her knees would give out under her. How she heard the question over the roaring in her ears defied explanation. "No," she said weakly. "That's quite all right, Ms. Bayliss."

He smiled at Deirdre, who looked far from reassured, and practically shut the door in her face. Jessica wobbled to her desk and virtually collapsed into her chair. "Well, Morgan," she squeaked, with a pathetic lack of originality, "it's you."

"In the flesh," he said, his gaze swinging around the room to take in the mahogany furnishings, the credentials hanging on the wall, the magnolia framed in the French windows that led to the quadrangle, and coming to rest finally on her.

Oh, in the flesh, indeed! Every gorgeous, formal inch of him! No blue jeans today, no stetson, no leather boots, but a tailored navy blazer, grey pants, white shirt and ultra-conservative burgundy tie. The dark, unruly hair was combed into submission, the jaw freshly shaven. And the face, the eyes, the mouth....

Jessica swallowed helplessly and pressed her knees together so hard that the little bones on the inside of her ankles ground painfully against each other. "Well," she said again, and followed that up with the most inane question of all time. "Are you here to register your daughter?"

He subjected her to a long, level stare. "No. To the best of my knowledge, I don't have a daughter—or a son, either."

"Of course not," she said. "I remember now you told me there were no children from your marriage."

"Is that all you remember about me, Jessica?" he asked gently.

"No," she whispered, the same old awareness arcing between them again, a high-voltage wire dangerously alive. "I remember everything. *Everything.* Especially your fear that commitment to your work would prove an insurmountable obstacle to our finding happiness together."

She chanced another direct glance at the handsome, unsmiling face and all her self-protective instincts converged to shield her from yet another disappointment. From habit, the headmistress supplanted the lover—unimpeachably correct, starchily aloof. "Which makes me wonder, Morgan, why you're here now. Have you decided to give up the law and be what you once led me to believe you were—a simple rancher with no hidden agenda?"

He paced to the window and stared out. "I've thought about it," he said, his smoky, sexy voice playing sonatas down her spine. "I've indulged in endless games of 'what if' over the last few months."

He swung around to face her and she marveled that she somehow managed to stop herself from rushing to him and flinging herself into his arms. But she dared not, not until she knew for sure....

"I wondered if we could handle a long-distance marriage, with you here and me someplace else—the ranch, or private practice, perhaps. Such marriages sometimes work," he said, at her small exclamation of protest.

"Not for me," she said firmly.

He drummed his fingertips on the window ledge. "I see."

"Really?" She moistened her lips with the tip of her tongue. "And what is it that you see, Morgan?"

"You've done what I haven't been able to do. You've put the past—our past—behind you."

"And how," she inquired, the headmistress still refusing to bow out and let the woman who loved him speak from her heart, "do you arrive at that conclusion?"

"Well, hell," he said, his voice raw with misery, "I think I just proposed. And I know damn well you shot me down before I barely got the words out."

The warmth that was melting her heart stole into her face, softening her features and thawing the tears damming her eyes. She blinked them away. "I didn't mean to do that. What else did you wish to say?"

He heaved a great sigh. "That I was wrong to let you go, wrong to think time or distance would solve anything. That neither of those things has anything to do with love."

He flexed his shoulders and loosened the knot in his tie. "That the few days we shared, Jessica, have overshadowed every waking minute of the last three and a half months for me. That I tried to forget you—for your sake, for mine—"

He stopped again and raked his fingers through his hair, disheveling its tidy perfection. "Hell, I don't know! And what does it matter anyway, if you don't feel—?"

She couldn't bear it a minute longer, not the pain they'd both suffered, not the time they'd wasted, and most especially not the stretch of carpet separating them that neither dared to cross. They were both so tentative, so cautious, so protective—of each other, of themselves.

One of them had to be brave and he'd already laid himself on the line for her. It was her turn to take a chance.

"I won't settle for a long-distance marriage," she said, at last finding the strength to do what she'd wanted to do from the moment she'd seen him standing in her office doorway. Pushing herself out of her chair, she went to him and put her arms around his waist. "If I love a man enough to marry him, I want to be with him all the time."

"Do you still love me, Jessica?"

"Oh, yes," she whispered, leaning her head against his chest. "I thought the feelings might die, especially when I didn't hear from you, but they didn't. I've missed you so much, Morgan."

"Me too," he said, wrapping his arms around her. "Me too, sweetheart."

"If being a rancher full-time will make you happy...?"

"It won't," he said. "That's Clancy's idyll, not mine. Speaking of whom, there's one man who'll happily dance at our wedding. I think he'd marry you himself if he had the chance. But about that other 'what if' I mentioned—the one about going into private practice—"

"Is that what you really want, Morgan?"

"No." She felt the shuddered intake of his breath, sensed the battle he was waging within himself. He tightened his arms around her. "You're a remarkable human being, and I love you for who you are, for the way you think. But more than that I need you. Don't make me go the distance alone, Jessica. My work—it's not always pretty, it's seldom polite and it's almost..." he drew a deep, despairing breath "...almost never clean. But it's who I am, what I believe in, and if I'm to go on making a difference—trying to make things better—I have to have someone to come home to who believes in me. I have to have you."

"You already do," she said. "I've been yours for the taking for months."

"But I don't have the right." He gestured at the elegant office with its white-painted classical fireplace and high coved ceiling. "How can I ask you to give up the ordered, exclusive life you've carved out for yourself here? Because that's what it really boils down to, sweetheart. I can't be effective as a crown prosecutor living on Springhill Island."

"But I can be a wife anywhere."

"You'd do that? You'd give up your job just to be with me?"

She would have laughed if she hadn't been so close to tears. "*Just* to be with you? Morgan, my dearest love, I left here at Christmas believing I was a whole woman but I knew, by the time I came back, that I'd brought only half of me home."

She touched his face, tracing loving fingers over his cheek, his jaw, his mouth. "Teaching, running this school—I made them my life because they were all I had and for a long time they were enough. But then there was you, and everything changed. With you, finer dreams didn't seem so impossible any more."

"Why didn't you tell me? We've wasted so much time."

"I wasn't willing to risk having you turn away from me. I thought, on Christmas night when you left me outside that service station, that I'd never felt such heartache, and I made a vow I'd never leave myself open to that sort of pain again. But I've learned there are worse things."

"Are there?" he said tenderly, lowering himself to the chair she'd recently vacated. "Such as what?"

"Such as being a prisoner of one's pride. Such as

being afraid to live. Would you believe," she said, allowing him to draw her down onto his lap, "that I decided this afternoon that it was time I stopped being such a coward? I was going to come to you and refuse to go away unless you could tell me you were happier without me. Because you can't turn off love, no matter how ill advised it might seem, no matter how inconvenient."

"There could be other Gabriel Parrishes, sweetheart."

"If there are, we'll face them together. It's time to close old doors, Morgan, especially with so many new ones waiting to be opened. I'm not Daphne; you're not Stuart."

He took her face between his two hands. "I don't know how I lived without you, my lovely Jessica, but I do know I can't go on that way. Will you marry me, despite everything?"

"No," she sighed as his mouth inched toward hers. "I'll marry you because of everything."

EPILOGUE

"HELLO, gal. Sorry I haven't been up to chat the last few days but I've been away to the coast, to a weddin'. Morgan's weddin', Agnes, and you ain't seen nothin' like it. More fancy folks in fancy clothes than you could shake a stick at. An' queer food like you wouldn't believe. Weren't at all sure a man were meant to put it in his mouth, let alone swallow the dad-blamed stuff. Nothin' like your good home cookin', gal. And the drink—hah! Fizzed up a man's nose worse'n that mornin' brew you used to concoct to keep me regular through the winter.

"But it were worth the trip, just to see Morgan so happy. And that Jessica! Why, Agnes, she looked darn near as beautiful as you did the day you married me. All in white, she were, with the rear end of her dress trailin' behind her for half a mile. You'd've loved all the flowers, gal. Roses and sweet-smellin' foreign things, and little white misty bits of stuff like the wild baby's breath you used to grow, 'cept this were bigger and come from a greenhouse.

"As for Morgan, well, he'd've looked just fine if he could've kept the sappy grin off his face. Embarrassing, it were, watchin' him. Good thing he got himself a sensible wife this time. She'll do, Agnes. She's a good woman—could've been your daughter if God had seen fit to send us one. Feet planted on the ground and good-hearted, that's the new Mrs. Kincaid. She'll not be runnin' for the hills at the first sign of trouble. She'll deal with it, just the way you would've.

"Reckon there'll be young'uns before long, gal. Jessica turned all red in the face when I asked and Morgan

188

told me to hush my mouth. Said it weren't something he wanted broadcast just yet, as though a little foal were already bakin' in the oven. Wouldn't surprise me a bit, Agnes, the way he carried on at Christmas, sniffin' around her all the time. Thought I was goin' to have to hog-tie him to the stable door a couple of times.

"He and his new missus is comin' up to the ranch in September. I'll introduce you then and, come next spring, I'll bet my last dollar there'll be a baby to show off.

"Anyway, gal, there it is, all the news that's fit to print. I missed you. I always do when I'm away from you. Reckon I can understand how Morgan feels. When the right woman comes along, she makes a man feel whole.

"Best be gettin' back to work now. The wild flowers is bloomin' all around you, all red and orange and purple, just the way you always wanted. You rest easy and I'll stop by again tomorrow, same as always. I've loved you for nearly fifty years, darlin'. I ain't about to stop now."

Coming Next Month

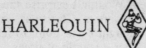

HARLEQUIN PRESENTS®

THE BEST HAS JUST GOTTEN BETTER!

#1929 A MARRIAGE TO REMEMBER Carole Mortimer
Three years ago Adam Carmichael had walked out on Maggi—now he was back! Divorce seemed the only way to get him out of her life for good. But Adam wasn't going to let her go without a fight!

#1930 RED-HOT AND RECKLESS Miranda Lee
(Scandals!)
Ben Sinclair just couldn't put his schoolboy obsession with Amber behind him. She *still* thought she could have anything because she was rich and beautiful. But now Ben had a chance to get even with her at last....

#1931 TIGER, TIGER Robyn Donald
Leo Dacre was determined to find out what had happened to his runaway half brother, but Tansy was just as determined not to tell him! It was a clash of equals...so who would be the winner?

#1932 FLETCHER'S BABY Anne McAllister
Sam Fletcher never ran away from difficult situations, so when Josie revealed that she was expecting his child, marriage seemed the practical solution. And he wasn't going to take no for an answer!

#1933 THE SECRET MOTHER Lee Wilkinson
(Nanny Wanted!)
Caroline had promised herself that one day she would be back for Caitlin. Now, four years later, she's applying for the job of her nanny. Matthew Carran, the interviewer, doesn't *seem* to recognize her. But he has a hidden agenda....

#1934 HUSBAND BY CONTRACT Helen Brooks
(Husbands and Wives)
For Donato Vittoria, marriage was a lifetime commitment. Or so Grace had thought—until she'd discovered his betrayal, and fled. But in Donato's eyes he was still her husband, and he wanted her back in his life—and in his bed!

HARLEQUIN PRESENTS®

Follow your heart, not your head,
in our exciting series:

—when passion knows no reason...

Watch for these dramatic stories about women who know
the odds are against them—but dare to risk it all!

November 1997—
A GUILTY AFFAIR (#1920)
by Diana Hamilton

December 1997—
CHRISTMAS WITH A STRANGER (#1927)
by Catherine Spencer

Available wherever Harlequin books are sold.

Look us up on-line at: http://www.romance.net   FORB497

HARLEQUIN PRESENTS®

How could any family be complete without a nineties nanny?

NANNY WANTED!

...as a friend, as a parent or even as a partner...

A compelling new series from our bestselling authors about nannies whose talents extend way beyond looking after the children:

January 1998—THE SECRET MOTHER
by Lee Wilkinson (#1933)

February 1998—THE LOVE-CHILD
by Kathryn Ross (#1938)

March 1998—A NANNY NAMED NICK
by Miranda Lee (#1943)

April 1998—A NANNY IN THE FAMILY
by Catherine Spencer (#1950)

P.S. Remember, nanny knows best when it comes to falling in love!

Available wherever Harlequin books are sold.

Look us up on-line at: http://www.romance.net   HPRNNY1